Secret Paradise

DARA GIRARD

KIMANI™
ROMANCE

KIMANI PRESS™

Recycling programs
for this product may
not exist in your area.

ISBN-13: 978-0-373-86250-4

SECRET PARADISE

Copyright © 2012 by Sade Odubiyi

www.kimanipress.com

Printed in U.S.A.

Dear Reader,

Have you ever wanted to get away from it all? The obligations, the job that no longer excites you, the on-again, off-again boyfriend you should have broken up with months ago? That's exactly how Nikki Dupree feels when she impulsively takes an assignment to redesign the house of the reclusive Lucian Kontos.

Initially, I thought Nikki would have fun with JD's brother from *All I Want Is You*. But they were having too much fun and nothing was happening so I had to go with someone who could prove a challenge to her. Enter JD's friend Lucian.

Immediately, an electricity ignites between them that seems to expand to everything and everyone around them. An attraction so powerful that even the gods and goddesses of myth seem to take a hand in it....

So, my dear reader, here is another tale I hope you enjoy.

Dara Girard

Prologue

He would die tonight in this hell of his own creation. Flames licked at the walls outside his bedroom, shattering the windows down the hall, and turning everything they touched into blackened ash. Everything burned around him and he would soon burn with it. The fire had yet to reach the room where he'd imprisoned himself, but he knew the smoke would take him first. He imagined gossamer black arms seeping under the door, slowly gathering together to strangle him. Lucian Kontos let the smoke invade his lungs, just as he'd let Alana invade his life and his heart.

Even now he could see her face, remember the scent of her lotion, the seductive fragrance of her perfume, the touch of her hand, the beautiful slope of her neck when she threw her head back and laughed. She loved to laugh. It was what had attracted him to her at first. Now he wondered if she'd been laughing at him. It seemed likely now, as he looked back. He'd been a fool. Not only because he'd carelessly let her into every part of his life, but because he'd given her his heart as well. That had made him as weak and blind as a newborn puppy. God, how he'd loved her, and now he'd die because of it. But he welcomed this end. His shame demanded this punishment. It suited his sense of honor and justice. His foolish heart had led him to a fiery grave.

Lucian inhaled the smoke, waiting for the toxins to slowly suffocate him and turn his lungs as black as charcoal, and prepared for death.

"Uncle Lucian!"

The urgent voice of a young girl ripped through the loud roar of the flames. A distant cry that he hadn't expected to hear.

"Uncle Lucian!"

No, not a cry. A scream. She was screaming for him. *Callia.* But she wasn't supposed to be here. She was to be safely away. Miles away. He'd made sure his brother took her with him. Maybe he was hallucinating. Yes, that was it. He was having an auditory hallucination because she was the one thing he truly regretted having to leave behind. But he'd made sure she would be taken care of.

"Uncle Lucian!"

Lucian stiffened in the chair where he'd been awaiting his end and swore. He wasn't hallucinating. She was here in this inferno he'd once called his home, screaming his name. Instantly the sweet call of death and its promises to end all his suffering no longer mattered. He had to save Callia. He had to reach her. He grabbed a pillowcase and covered his mouth, then went to the door, ignoring the pain in his leg, and opened it. He dropped to his knees so that he could crawl under the layer of black smoke that choked the air. He knew the smoke would overtake them both, so there wasn't much time to reach her.

"Uncle Lucian!"

He wanted to call out and let her know that he was coming to get her, that he'd do anything to make sure she was safe, but he knew that he couldn't. He had to reserve what little oxygen he had left.

Lucian reached the stairs and saw the bright glow of the red, orange and yellow flames below and heard her voice again, but he still couldn't see where she was. He was about to turn away when he saw something wiggle on the floor. That was when he noticed her fingers. He rushed forward and saw Callia hanging from the edge of one of the steps where a staircase used to stand.

"Callia!"

She looked up, her eyes wide with terror. It mirrored his own—as if they'd found each other locked together in purgatory—but he quickly replaced his fear with a steely determination. She would not die. He wouldn't think of the long drop that awaited her if she fell or the flames that shot up to seize her.

"I can't hold on," she said.

"You must hold on to me." He grabbed the railing, praying for it to hold, and wrapped an arm around her neck. He straightened, then grabbed her around the waist as the stair fell away. There was no way out except up. He lifted her in his arms and dashed toward a room off to the side and closed the door, knowing they didn't have much time before the fire reached them.

He pounded his fist against the door, then turned to her. "You're not supposed to be here."

She wrapped her arms around herself. "I sensed something was wrong and I told Basilio."

"And he brought you back here?" Lucian said, angered that his younger brother would ignore his orders. He'd come back into his life only eight months ago, after nearly a decade of separation. "Where is he?"

"He's not here."

"Then who brought you here?"

"I don't know."

"You have to know," Lucian said, pressing her, eager for details. The information she knew was vital to him. "You didn't get here by magic."

"I really don't know how I got here. I woke up in my room and smelled the smoke. At first I thought I was dreaming."

Lucian pounded the door again. It was even worse than he'd imagined. Someone must have drugged her and placed her in the house, knowing what was going to happen. But why? "When you woke up, you should have tried to escape."

"But I had to find you first to warn you. I knew you were in danger."

He gritted his teeth. "That's why you should have stayed away."

Callia blinked and he saw the tears. He rarely lost his temper with her, but he couldn't comfort her now. She was only eleven but already had her mother's beauty and her father's defiant nature. Now wasn't the time to argue. Silence was better. He needed to think. He walked toward a set of windows and winced as a shooting pain ripped through his side, making him feel as if he'd aged a hundred years.

Callia took a step toward him. "You're hurt."

Lucian held his hand out, keeping her away. "I'm

fine," he lied. Yes, he hurt. He hurt all over, as if every nerve ending had been electrified, but that didn't matter now. He needed to keep her safe. Lucian opened one of the windows and lifted her onto the windowsill. "I'm going to throw you into the pool."

She shook her head. "No."

"There's no reason to be afraid. It will be okay."

"I want you to come with me. Let's jump together."

"No need. You know how to swim." He lifted her up.

She grabbed the window frame. "No."

"Callia, listen to me."

She fought him even harder. "No!"

"You must jump," he demanded, struggling with her.

"No!" she screamed. Her resistance was just as frantic as when he'd found her on the stairs, clinging for her life.

He released his hold and stared at her, bewildered. "Why not?"

"If you let me go, you won't come with me."

Lucian silently swore, hung his head and released a heavy sigh. She knew him too well. Sometimes he wondered why this strange little girl loved him so much. Especially since he was the cause of her father's death.

He lifted his head and met her eyes, his voice stern. "Callia, you are going to listen to me." He cupped her face in his hands. He'd never pleaded in his life, but this time he would for her sake. "My little one. Please listen to me. Your life is all I treasure. Save it for me."

"No. Either I live with you or I die with you."

A part of him wanted to laugh at her bold statement, and another part wanted to shake her. This skinny little thing who was all arms and legs wanted to fight *him?* He could easily overpower her, and if he had more strength, he would have by now. He knew he could crush her body, but not her will. He heard the roar of the flames at the door and saw fear enter her eyes. She didn't want to die, despite her rash claim, and she didn't deserve to.

She grabbed the front of his shirt in her tiny fist. "Come on, Uncle Lucian. Let's go." She tightened her grip. "Jump with me."

"We don't have time for this."

She buried her face in his neck. "Please, Uncle Lucian. Please don't leave me alone."

"You won't be alone. You'll have—"

She vigorously shook her head and said in a trembling voice, "No, please. Please!"

"Shh. Don't cry." He sighed. "Okay. I'll jump after you."

She shook her head again.

"I promise."

"You promise, really?" She held out her hand.

He took it and held it against his chest, over his heart. "I promise. On my soul." He kissed her hand, then released it. "Now, let's go."

She looked at him.

He turned her face. "Don't look back at me. Only look ahead. Remember what I taught you?"

"Where I'm going matters more than where I've been," she said, as though repeating a solemn vow.

"Right."

She hugged him. "I love you, Uncle Lucian."

"I know," he said impatiently, disentangling himself from her grasp. They didn't have time. He had to get her to safety. "Face forward."

She did, and he threw her out the window and watched her fall into the water. He waited for her to emerge to the surface and felt his tense heart relax when he saw her head pop up and she swam to the edge of the Olympic-size pool. She was safe.

The fire was at the door. Lucian could hear it pressing against the wood, wanting entrance. He turned to the door, knowing that in an instant it could all be over. All the secrets, betrayal and curses could die with him. It was his fate. He turned to the window from which Callia had fallen, and stared at the darkening sky, watching as the sinking sun created the same violent reds and yellows against the horizon as the blaze that consumed his house. He'd promised Callia he would live, even though she'd be better off without him. He'd promised on his soul, but he felt he had no soul to make a promise with. Looking down, he saw her mouth move, but it was too distant to hear. He knew she was calling his name.

He wouldn't leave her yet; he'd defy fate. He sat on the edge of the window. "I'm coming," he said, not caring if she heard him or not. He would not leave her afraid. Just as he was pushing away from the windowsill to launch into the air, the fire broke through the door and reached through the room like the long arm of a fiery beast, as if trying to grab him back. Glass exploded above him and the uncontrolled fire continued to fuel itself. Then suddenly there was an explosion caused by a back draft, the result of the fire suddenly receiving oxygen, and it propelled Lucian through the air.

Before he hit the water, he briefly wondered if he'd have a watery grave instead of a fiery one, and then he thought of nothing else.

Chapter 1

Dear God, how was he going to tell her? J. D. Rozan set his phone down and shut off his computer, trying to strategize how best to break the news to his wife.

Monica knew about tragedy. Her first husband had died in a vicious incident, and she'd survived a past that would have sent another type of woman to a mental ward. He'd wanted to protect her from any more pain, but that seemed impossible. The last three years had been perfect. Nothing to mar their idyllic existence at the farmhouse in Georgia. J.D. looked out the window and saw the red flash of a cardinal as it flew past. He thought of their daughter, Starla, who was napping in the upstairs nursery. She was a happy child who giggled at the sound of thunderstorms and loved to jump into puddles. This lazy summer day he'd taken time off because Monica's sister, Nikki, had come to visit and he planned to take them all to the beach. But that would have to change.

J.D. pushed himself from his chair and left the room he used as a study. He had to tell her. He'd just have to do it fast. He took a deep breath and walked toward his wife's studio, where she designed jewelry for her clients around the world. J.D. stood in front of the door and raised his hand to knock, then hesitated when he heard Monica's laughter, followed by her sister's. J.D. let his hand fall. He could tell her later, at dinner or before they went to bed, but then he didn't know how much time there was left. She needed to know now. He sighed, then knocked.

"Come in."

J.D. stepped into the bright, airy studio. He saw his wife and stopped. She was so beautiful that even the sun seemed to seek her out in the room, its tender rays stroking her long, straight black river of hair, caressing her exquisite profile and highlighting her gorgeous eyes. She greeted him with a smile, which always made him want to kiss her. Her younger sister, Nikki, sat in the shadowed corner near the window, wearing jeans and a peasant blouse, with her hair pulled back in a ponytail sporting two silver streaks. She wasn't as striking as her sister, but she had a unique beauty all her own, sharp hazel eyes and a pug nose. There was no envy between the sisters, just an acceptance similar to how the moon made way for the sun. J.D. was glad she was there.

He took a deep breath and shoved his hands in his pockets. "Monica." That was all he said. He'd never know if it was the tone or his expression, but something made her drop her tools.

She ran over to him, her eyes wide with fear. "What happened?"

He led her over to a chair. "Sit down."

She pulled away from him. "Just tell me."

"It's Lucian."

She collapsed into the chair. "He's dead?"

"Nearly. At this point it's touch and go. The doctors are doing everything they can for him."

"What happened?" Nikki asked when her sister remained silent.

"An explosion at his mansion caused a massive fire, and he and Callia were trapped inside and barely escaped. He was badly burned. They had to put him into a coma. His brother Basilio just called me. He wants us to be prepared in case…"

Monica shook her head. "He's strong." She returned to her drafting table, as if everything was settled. J.D. shared a look with Nikki. If she wanted to be in denial, who was he to stop her?

Nikki frowned. "Monica, you can't pretend that he may not make it."

Monica spun around and glared at her sister. "I'm not pretending anything. I know Lucian Kontos and I know that a man like him will live."

Nikki rolled her eyes. "Monica—"

"No."

J.D. shook his head. "Honey—"

Monica looked at him, her lips pursed. "He'll get through this." She pointed a pencil at him. "When we went to his island for our honeymoon, I was still having nightmares about my past and couldn't stop. Do you know what he said? He said that if anything ever happened to you, he'd take care of me. That I was his family, too, and it was real. He sees you as a brother. You can't give up on him."

J.D. threw up his hands in frustration. "I'm not giving up on him. I've known him for years. I love him as much as you do, but I know about his injuries. He's been badly burned. This is a man who loves life, and all that it has to offer. He'll be undergoing several surgeries, but we have to admit that in spite of all the therapy and plastic surgery he may be able to afford, there's still a limitation to what medicine can do. He may not regain the use of his arm or ever walk again. Even if he lives, he won't be the same man."

"He'll recover," Monica said defiantly.

J.D. folded his arms and looked grim.

Nikki stiffened. "There's something else you're not telling us."

J.D. nodded. "It's about the explosion. They think it was arson."

"Someone tried to kill him?" Monica asked.

"They're investigating. His brother is looking into all possibilities."

"I'm sure it was a simple accident," Nikki said, reading the look of horror on Monica's face.

Monica shook her head. "That house is enormous. He should have had time to escape."

"Fires move fast," Nikki said.

"Mama?" a tiny voice said through the baby monitor.

Nikki stood. "I'll get her," she said quickly, then left before anyone could argue.

Monica watched her sister go, then returned her gaze to J.D. "Are you going to see him?"

"When I can. He's in a secret location, and I'll wait for word from his brother when it seems safe."

"Call him back and tell him to tell Lucian about the baby."

J.D. searched her face, confused. "The baby? What baby?"

She took his hand and placed it on her stomach. "Ours."

"You're pregnant?"

She winked.

For a moment J.D. just stared at her, not knowing what to say or even how to feel. At first he felt an almost intoxicating joy; then, as he thought of his friend, guilt and sadness mingled with it.

"He's in a coma," J.D. said in a grave tone. "There's no point."

"But part of him may hear. The part that wants to live." Monica caressed the side of his face. "He will live."

J.D. gathered her close. He closed his eyes, determined to believe her—feeling her warmth and strength and courage. She was right. Lucian was a tough SOB. He would rise like the phoenix.

"Good job!" Nikki said, clapping her hands when Starla threw a stick for the family dog, Baxter, to retrieve. It had barely gone a foot, but Nikki acted as if little Starla had the makings of a javelin thrower. Starla giggled, delighting in her aunt's praise, and Baxter picked up the stick, his tail wagging. They played in the front yard, where Nikki had taken them after Starla's nap. She enjoyed being in the outdoors, especially on warm summer days like this. Were she alone, she would be lazing on the porch with a cool glass of iced tea.

"Now it's my turn," she said when Baxter dropped

the stick at her feet. She picked it up and threw it far enough to give the dog some exercise.

"Good job!" a voice said behind her.

Nikki turned and saw her sister coming out of the house. She held up a hand. "Stop right there."

Monica paused, puzzled. "What?"

"Do I know you from somewhere? You look vaguely familiar. Has anyone ever told you that you should model?" Nikki chuckled as she took a seat on the porch step.

Monica made a face. "Shut up," she said in good humor.

"Don't you sometimes miss those days?" Nikki asked, referring to her sister's past as a top fashion model.

Monica sat on the porch step above hers. "No. When I'm here, I feel richer than I've ever been."

Nikki could see it. Her sister glowed with good health and happiness. "I'm glad."

"I'm sorry I snapped at you earlier."

Nikki shrugged. "Wouldn't be the first time we argued about a man."

Monica lowered her head and Nikki fell silent, because they both knew that was true. Nikki had never taken to Monica's first husband, Delong Price, who'd whisked Monica away and launched her as the international beauty named Venus: a symbol of sex, glamour and elegance. But now those days were over. Nikki looked around her. Her sister and J.D. owned a slice of heaven here. They called it a farmhouse, but over the years it had expanded into a magnificent piece of architecture, while retaining its wholesome feel and charm. Nikki found herself spending any free moment she could find visiting her sister and her family.

She'd never been this close to her sister since they were children. Delong had liked to keep Monica to himself, and if she wasn't with him, she was working. Now she had her own business and a more relaxed schedule and a man who let her be completely herself. Nikki liked J.D. At first glance she wouldn't have selected him for Monica. He was handsome, with the cool command of a businessman and the slight ruthlessness that went with it, but she'd never seen that side of him. Only kindness. At times Nikki imagined meeting her own J.D. but always brushed the thought aside. Her sister's life could never be hers. She did wonder about Lucian though. Anytime J.D. or Monica talked about him, she found herself listening closer. He intrigued her. She knew he'd come to visit a few times, but they always seemed to miss each other. Monica had once mentioned that Lucian had commented on her design skills.

They'd allowed her to infuse the farmhouse with their African American and Native American heritage, and she'd used aging cedar, with ancestral images hand carved into the walls. The front door featured unique symbols of good fortune, but she'd learned what Lucian liked most were the series of retractable skylights she put in the family room. She would have liked to find out what else he'd like, but now it seemed she might never get the chance to meet him.

Baxter returned and dropped the stick in front of them. Monica picked it up and threw it. Starla giggled and Nikki clapped and said in mocking tones, "Good job! Beautiful and strong."

Monica playfully punched her in the arm. "You're a nuisance."

Nikki rested back on her elbows and looked up at the sky. "Did you tell him about the baby?"

"Yes, just a few minutes ago."

Nikki looked at her, curious. "How did he take it?"

"He's thrilled."

"I would have waited until another time."

Monica shrugged. "I know J.D. He needed something to smile about. He's really worried about Lucian."

"I hope your friend makes it."

Monica pulled a picture out of her pocket and handed it to her. "This is his house."

Nikki took the photograph and stared at the expansive mansion. "I know. You showed it to me before." She'd been amazed by the honeymoon photos Monica had shown her of Lucian's island. Lush, romantic, exclusive. She would have loved the chance to see inside his house. But she'd never been bold enough to invite herself. However, although there were pictures of the island and mansion, there were none of the man. In one photo she'd seen a shadowy figure in the background, but it had been too blurry to make out any features. Monica had told her Lucian didn't like to have his photo taken and kept to himself.

Nikki handed the photo back to Monica, confused as to why her sister had given it to her. "Most of it has been burned, right?"

"Yes, he's going to need to rebuild."

"I'm sure he will."

"And redesign it."

Nikki frowned, suspicious. "Where are you going with this?"

"He's going to need you."

Nikki laughed. "Me? Why me?"

"Because you're the best."

Nikki smiled. "And?"

"And what?"

Nikki narrowed her eyes. "You're up to something."

"His place is awe-inspiring."

"So is the Taj Mahal."

"Once you get to know him—"

Nikki shook her head. "I'm seeing someone already."

"I saw the way you looked at his house."

"Because it's amazing."

Monica smiled. "Wait until you meet the man."

Chapter 2

Four years later

"You bitch!"

Nikki heard the shattering glass just as she entered her office.

"You need to stop looking in the mirror."

Nikki ducked as a handcrafted vase she'd purchased in Peru went flying past her. She straightened and saw two finely groomed women ready to pulverize each other. Only minutes ago she'd received a frantic call from her assistant, Abby Lagoria, that she had an unexpected guest in her office. The tone of the call had surprised her because usually Abby was unflappable. She was a woman who had the kind of face suited for a cubicle. Non-smiling, dreary and forgettable, but Nikki had hired her because she was efficient. She had a remarkable ability to get things done. No one canceled on

her, and bills were always paid. Nothing seemed beyond
her capabilities—until now. Evidently here was a situation beyond her. This was a crisis.

The mistress of Senator Allwater had shown up
without an appointment. Nikki never saw clients or potential clients without an appointment. It was the best
way to train people in how to treat her. She'd discovered
early on that you couldn't be too available to the upper
class, or they'd devalue you. Exclusivity was a must.
And she was very exclusive. Unfortunately, the usually
refined Meredith Weedon had broken protocol, and so
had Elissa Gold, Allwater's second mistress. They'd
come to her office, both laying claim to the newly designed apartment he'd paid for.

Meredith, his first mistress, was almost an exact
replica of Allwater's wife: old money and new breasts.
His second mistress was a midlife crisis cliché—early
twenties, tight clothes and big earrings. She had an
expensive beauty that would grow more costly as she
aged, because she likely wouldn't age well. She was
reckless with her skin care and smoked and drank as
if they were a dietary requirement. But she was young
enough to keep the consequences of her behavior at bay,
for at least a decade.

Meredith was no less expensive, just better at main-
taining herself. Good breeding and care had given her
an advantage, but while Meredith was more sophisticated, Elissa was more clever than she looked. Allwater
usually kept them separate. The fact that they were both
here meant that something had gone terribly wrong.

Meredith flicked back a strand of blond hair, her
hand trembling with anger. "I was with him first and
have known him a lot longer than you."

Elissa's full, pouty mouth spread into a cold smile.

"Honey, every man eventually likes to get a younger model."

"New toys always get replaced."

Elissa's smile fell and she picked up a glass statue of two swans in the shape of a heart.

Nikki had had enough. "Put that down," she said. She saw Elissa's mouth kick up in a quick malicious grin. "Drop it and I'll throw a punch that will have you flying through that window."

Elissa blinked, surprised by Nikki's violent threat, and slowly set the statue down when she realized from Nikki's stance that she wasn't bluffing. "Who are you?"

"The owner of this place," Abby said, disgusted by the woman's ignorance.

"Oh, the decorator."

"The designer," Nikki corrected.

"She wouldn't know the difference," Meredith said with disdain.

Elissa narrowed her eyes. "I know the difference between a cow and a heifer."

"Sure you do, dear. They were your parents," Meredith returned.

Nikki spoke up before Elissa lunged at Meredith. "Now, let's be civil." She stepped forward and winced at the sound of crunching glass beneath her feet. "I think we can come up with a compromise. There's enough room to accommodate both of you. I will create two entirely separate apartments—each with its own entrance—and will design your own special space to reflect you intimately, a space that will keep your favorite playboy entertained for life." She knew she'd hit on the perfect solution when Meredith began asking for a gazillion mirrors and chandeliers, while Elissa requested items for a "naughty" lair to call her own. She

recorded their requests and made two separate appoint-
ments for further discussion. "Consider it done. I'll let
Angelo know that I'll be making some changes," she
said, using Allwater's code name.

After the two women left, Nikki collapsed into her
chair.

"I'm so sorry," Abby said, glancing around the room.
"They just showed up and then—"

"It's okay. It's not your fault."

Her phone rang and Abby answered. She put it on
hold and turned to Nikki. "It's Benjamin."

Nikki groaned. Benjamin Leano was a bad habit
she needed to break. She thought of coming up with
an excuse not to talk to him, then sighed and held out
her hand. Abby gave her the phone, then left the room.

"You're in town?" she said, trying not to sound
bored.

"Yes," he said, surprised. "How did you know?"

It wasn't a hard deduction. He called her only when
he was in town. He was a photojournalist who traveled
the world but managed to remember her whenever he
was in New York. Two years ago it had seemed like a
great arrangement, but now it was wearing thin. "Just
a guess."

"What's wrong? You sound distracted."

She looked around her office at the broken vases,
the glass, the crooked picture and the tilted plant. She
briefly shut her eyes, feeling the slight pounding of an
oncoming headache. "Client issues."

"Poor baby. Let me take you out."

"That sounds good, but I'm busy." She pinched the
bridge of her nose. "This isn't working."

"I'll wait if you need to switch phones."

"Not the lines, us."

He paused. "You want something more? Marriage? Fine. I'll marry you."

Nikki laughed at his flippant attitude. "No, I don't want to marry you."

"Why not?"

"Benjamin, you don't want to get married."

"That's not the point. Why wouldn't you want to marry me? I'm a great catch."

"Yes, for someone else."

"Are you interested in someone else? Are you seeing another man?"

"No, it's not that." She was just bored. Everything about her life had become routine. The wealthy clients and their tirades, the social events. There were no happy surprises or new discoveries. "I just need a break."

"We don't have to go to—"

"Sorry. I have another call I have to take. I'll call you later." She hung up before he could argue.

Abby came into the room, looking composed again. She straightened the tilted plant. "I've called housekeeping."

"Thank you."

"Is Benjamin stopping by?"

"No, never again."

"Good."

Nikki looked at her, shocked. "What do you mean?"

"You deserve better. When are you going to start designing your own home?"

"I've already designed my place."

Abby shook her head. "No, not a place. A home— with a fully furnished kitchen and a big family room."

"And a picket fence and lawn?" Nikki shook her

head and laughed. "You're talking to the wrong sister. That's not me."

"Everyone deserves their own space, where they feel complete."

"Right."

She knew that better than most. That was why she'd become a designer. She knew what a room could do, how it could make a person feel. But she didn't need a home of her own. She really liked her apartment and the friends and parties she hosted there. She was just restless. She only wished she knew what to do. She was young, attractive, with a good job and nothing really to complain about, yet she felt like running away.

Nikki stood. "What I need is a challenge. Something big and a little scary. Something to test my skills. Unpredictable." She looked around her destroyed office and groaned. She obviously wouldn't find it here. She needed the outdoors; she thought better there. "I'm going to go for a walk." She grabbed her bag and sunglasses.

Nikki walked several blocks, but the restless feeling still followed. She crossed over to go into Central Park. Then her phone rang. "Yes?" she said as she saw a driver give another the finger and a young child drop his ice cream on the pavement and burst into tears.

"It's Monica. Do you have a minute?"

"Sure." She stepped around a pile of dog poop someone had neglected to pick up. "What's up?"

"It's Lucian."

She stopped. "Has something happened? He's been out of the hospital for some time now and I thought he was doing fine."

"He is," Monica said quickly to reassure her.

"Good," Nikki said, starting to walk again. Over the past several years she'd become invested in Lucian's recovery. She'd been just as thankful as J.D. and Monica that he'd pulled through.

"This isn't a physical problem. It's his house. He's been able to rebuild, but the interior is a problem."

"I'm there," Nikki said without hesitation. This was the answer to her problems. She knew it. Already a sense of excitement had replaced her restlessness.

"You haven't let me finish."

"You don't need to finish," Nikki said, picking up her pace. If she were five years old, she would start to skip. "You need me to help him design his place, and I'm up to the challenge."

"I'm glad, but there are a few things you should know."

"I'll find out when I get there."

Monica hesitated. "He's not the easiest man to work with. Especially now. He uses a cane and J.D. says he can be very impatient and domineering."

Nikki brushed her sister's concerns aside. "I've dealt with that type before. Don't worry about me. I need a change and this is just the kind of project I was waiting for. Nothing can stop me from seizing this opportunity. Give me the details when I get home. I'll call you."

"But—"

"Bye." Nikki hung up the phone and released a little squeal of delight. This project was just what she needed. She'd finally get a chance to see inside the elusive Lucian Kontos's island mansion and meet the man. She wasn't sure which intrigued her more.

"Nikki!"

She spun around at the sound of her name and saw Benjamin running toward her. He was the kind of man who looked good in front of a camera and behind it. He had an easy smile and a great body. He moved with practiced grace, which made you feel comfortable around him. He was also the kind of man who was easy to say yes to, which was why Nikki hadn't broken up with him months ago.

"I'm so glad I found you," he said, giving her a quick hug.

Nikki stared at him, stunned, and annoyed that he felt and smelled so good. Whatever he asked her, she had to say no. "What are you doing here?"

"I was in the area when I called and I spoke to Abby and she told me you'd gone for a walk. I thought you'd end up here, but I wasn't sure."

Damn. Even her walks were routine. "Benjamin," she said slowly. "What are you doing here?"

"I'm doing what I should have done years ago." He got down on one knee. "Nikki—"

She tugged on his sleeve. "Get up. Don't do this," she said as some passersby stared.

"Marry me."

Nikki knelt in front of him. "I don't want to get married. I just got a great assignment and that's where my focus is right now. My career."

"We don't have to get married right away."

"Benjamin."

He seized her shoulders. "I don't want to lose what we have. It wasn't until this moment that I realized how much you mean to me." His brown eyes melted into hers. "Please say yes."

Saying yes to him had always been so easy. It had also been fun. She'd never regretted a moment. He was a good man. Could she get a better one? Could she find someone else who allowed her to have her own life?

Who didn't make demands on her time? Was it right to break up something just because she was bored? Maybe she was being too hasty. *Just say yes.* "Yes," she said, but the moment she did, her answer felt wrong. She didn't have the courage to take it back.

He kissed her. "I love you. We'll make each other happy." He grabbed her hand and slipped on a ring.

"Benjamin, wait," she said, amazed by the large stone. "I may have—"

"I know it's a big decision, but we'll make it work."

"How much did this cost you?"

"Doesn't matter. You're worth it, and I'll spend the rest of my life telling you so."

"This is all happening so fast." She started to take the ring off. "I can't say yes to this. Let me think some more."

Benjamin covered her hand. "No pressure. Just think of it as a gift and nothing else. I want you to wear it so that wherever you go, you'll think of me."

Nikki grinned. "Is that all?"

"No." His tone grew serious. "I want other men to know who your heart belongs to."

Her heart. Did her heart really belong to him? Had it ever belonged to anyone? It didn't matter. At least it was a change in their relationship, taking it to a deeper level, and she had to appreciate that. She wanted to tell him so, but her thoughts drifted to new island adventures, which she knew was her answer to everything.

Monica hung up the phone and stared at her husband, who was giving their son, Markos, named after the doctor who'd helped save Lucian's life, a piggyback ride, while their daughter, Starla, busied herself with her coloring book.

"Well, that was fast," J.D. said, surprised.

"She said she would do it."

"Did you tell her about—"

Monica shook her head and clasped her hands. "She wouldn't let me explain anything. She agreed before I even asked the question."

"So she doesn't know about—"

Monica shook her head again. "J.D., she doesn't care, and when Nikki wants something, nothing else matters. She's ready to do this."

"She's going to be in for a big surprise."

"Nikki can handle Lucian. I hope he can handle her."

J.D. grinned. "Lucian can handle anything."

"Did we just mix dynamite with gunpowder?"

J.D.'s grin grew. "All we can do is sit back and watch the fireworks."

Chapter 3

Yes, this was paradise. Nikki stood on the balcony, a slight breeze blowing the white cotton skirt she wore. It blended with the top she'd gotten from a local woman on the mainland. She'd stopped there for the day and roamed the market to get a feel of the culture. She saw some of the women wearing white skirts and patterned tops and asked one of them where she could purchase a similar outfit. The old lady in the store looked at Nikki, confused, so speaking in broken Greek and with a flash of money, she was able to make her request understood. The woman took the money, while still shaking her head, but left and came back with the two items Nikki wanted.

Nikki didn't care that the woman thought she was odd. She liked the loose-fitting style and wanted to feel a part of the land and culture and immerse herself in it. That meant shedding her typical New York clothes for bright colors and soft cotton fabrics that let her skin breathe. She turned her face to the warmth of the sun, which sat high in the cloudless blue sky. She loved the consistent warm weather, as well as the silence around her. She could actually hear her heart beating. There were no car fumes, flashing traffic lights or pounding footsteps on concrete.

The journey had been long, but she'd been treated like a queen—from her ride in Kontos's private jet to the luxury hotel on the mainland, where she stayed for a night until arrangements for transportation to the island could be made. There were only two ways to reach it: by boat or by helicopter. She'd first spotted the mansion as she sailed high over the water. As they approached the island, it came into view, the greenery seeming to make way for the soaring cliffs and the majestic structure, which appeared like a magical castle created out of the rock by a bolt of lightning from the gods. It was both wild and tamed, elegant and frightening. Nikki instantly fell in love.

She had never been in love before but could imagine these were the symptoms—racing heartbeat, breathlessness, a feeling as if she could float on a cloud. Yes, she was in love and she never wanted to come down. She stared at the magnificent structure with lust. There were so many things she could do. A feeling of rightness settled over her.

A driver met her once the helicopter had landed, and drove her to the mansion, which was even more amazing when seen from the ground, with its vine-laden steel balcony railings and sconces. This was where she was meant to be. When she was a little girl, she'd seen a postcard of a castle in Spain and imagined decorating every room. This was that dream coming true. Nikki rested her arms on the balcony railing and looked out at the landscape, spotting other villas along the cliffs and some down near the water. The wind carried the scent of the sea, which mingled with the aroma of fresh flowers. The island was a study in tranquility, but she couldn't say the same for the house. Once she'd stepped inside, she felt an emptiness. Despite the elaborately decorated hallways, the rooms she was hustled past were bare and sat neglected, with the eeriness of an empty tomb. Although the house had been rebuilt, there seemed to be a dark energy of melancholy that still lingered.

However, someone had taken care to make sure that her room was comfortable, with its expansive poster bed covered with expensive bedsheets and silk pillows, but that same care and attention hadn't gone into the rest of the house. She hadn't met the owner yet or Callia, but Nikki wasn't concerned. She knew there was plenty of time for that. She could just roam about a bit and get ideas.

Nikki had started to turn from the balcony when she glanced down and saw a man running, then another, followed by a third. Their movement and expressions told her that something was wrong. She went to the hallway and saw one of the household staff frantically grabbing a blanket.

"What's wrong?" she asked her.

"I don't know. I just have to get these," the woman said. Then her small, wiry figure hurried down the stairs and out the door.

Nikki followed. She wasn't as nimble as the woman as they made their way through the dense brush. Suddenly, the woman stopped and Nikki saw a crowd of people looking down into what appeared to be a tunnel. She glanced up and saw a man standing a few feet away. His back was turned to the excitement. Aside from his apparent disinterest, he was a hard figure to miss, dressed in light khaki trousers and an orange shirt, his hand gripping a wooden cane. But he leaned on it as if he didn't really need it. He wasn't what she'd expected. For a man who shied away from cameras, he looked like he would relish the attention.

Nikki walked over to him and then noticed the young woman by his side. She fit Monica's description of Callia. An older woman stood beside her and cast Nikki a curious glance but remained quiet.

"Mr. Kontos?" Nikki said, prepared to introduce herself.

He turned around.

Nikki blinked. He was beautiful. Exquisite. An Adonis dipped in honey. Every line of his face was perfection.

She held out her hand. "I'm Nikki Dupree."

He gave her hand a firm handshake and flashed a beautiful smile. "We were wondering when you'd get here. Sorry we didn't meet you at the house, but there's been an incident with one of the caves."

"Caves?" Nikki said with a frown. "It looks like a tunnel to me."

"This island is full of underground caves and tunnels, so be careful. Don't go and explore them, or you could end up dropping six feet down and could find yourself being swept out into the sea."

Nikki turned back to the crowd. "Is that what this is about? Someone fell in?"

"Yes," Callia said.

Kontos rolled his eyes. "Not someone. *Something.* Pauline. That's Callia's kitten."

"She threw her in," Callia said.

"I'm sure that's not true," Kontos said in an indulgent tone.

Callia scowled. "She hated cats."

"And she's not here. Don't make things up."

"I'm not making it up."

"Who are you talking about?" Nikki asked.

"The ghost," Callia replied.

Kontos waved his hand. "Ignore her."

"But I saw—"

"Quiet."

Callia shifted from one foot to the other. "Please let me go close and see—"

"No," the woman beside her said. "You're to stay right here."

"But—"

"Listen to Kay," Kontos said.

"I don't need a babysitter," Callia grumbled.

Nikki looked at the other woman, who was heavy-set, with a nervous energy. Her eyes shifted back and forth, as if they didn't know where to settle. Callia was going on fifteen now. That seemed old enough for her to look after herself. Why would she have a babysitter?

Nikki was about to ask why Callia thought someone had thrown her cat in when the young woman pointed with excitement.

"Look!"

Nikki turned and saw a massive form appear out of the cave—a head first, then gigantic forearms covered with muck and mud. Nikki gasped, remembering a horror film she'd once seen as a child about a swamp creature that had terrified a town. She knew he was a man, but he didn't look like one. He resembled some dark creature of brutish strength rising from the underworld. He had a large gash, with a thin stream of blood running from it, on the side of his head, and his cream shirt and dark trousers were soaking wet. But there was still something captivating about him that kept her gaze transfixed. He rested on his knees and reached inside his shirt and pulled out a little object. It looked like a drowned rat, but Nikki guessed it was Pauline. It lay lifeless on the ground.

"Poor thing," Kontos said with a sad shake of his head.

Callia cried out in despair and escaped his reassuring grasp. She pushed through the crowd and fell on her knees beside the body. "She killed her."

The other man silently picked up the kitten and blew into its mouth and nose and pumped its chest. It gasped, then threw up water, but remained limp in his large hands. The man began to rub it.

"What the hell is he doing?" Kontos said.

Nikki knew, but she also knew that his hands were too large to perform the delicate task. She pushed through the small crowd and took the kitten from him. She didn't know if he spoke English or not, but she didn't feel in the mood to explain herself. She knelt in front of him and rubbed the kitten, then shook it up and down. *Come on,* she silently prayed, hoping that she was doing it right. She'd once seen Monica's friend Treena, a veterinarian, do this on a runt puppy. Slowly she felt life returning, and the kitten opened its eyes and released a weak cry.

"You saved her!" Callia said, giving Nikki a quick hug. She kissed the other man on the cheek, took an offered towel and wrapped the kitten, then raced away. Kontos handed the man the wooden cane.

The man turned to Nikki. "Thanks for all your help,"

he said softly. He had ruggedly handsome features, ink-black hair, compelling green eyes, a hard mouth, and slowly a realization surfaced. Yes, this was the type of man who would stay in the shadows, who would shy away from photographs. His commanding stance was a clear indication that he was a man of power, used to having people follow his orders. She saw scars on his arm and another on his neck. This must be Lucian.

Nikki stared at him, knowing she should say something, but unable to get her lips to move. This was the man her sister had spoken about in such glowing terms? It had been a strange first encounter. Even though she couldn't speak, she forced her mouth into a smile.

That effort caught his attention and his piercing emerald eyes turned to her. "You must be the goddess Artemis," he said, his beautifully accented voice now taking on a husky tone. "You've made a young girl very happy. I know that it's customary to worship at your feet, but please allow me this one little exception." He drew her close and kissed her.

Nikki was too surprised to protest and expected to be disgusted by his bold action, but she wasn't. His mouth, which she'd only seconds ago thought hard, was as supple and sweet as melted caramel. Then, too soon, it was over, and he drew away, leaving her lips warm and tingling.

"Thank you," he said, his eyes blazing. "I'll make sure to get you a new uniform."

Nikki blinked. Her voice hoarse, she said, "Uniform?"

"Yes, your clothes are ruined."

Nikki glanced down at her blouse and skirt, which were covered in mud and muck. "Oh, that's okay. It was all for a good cause."

He stiffened, surprised. "You're American?"

"Yes."

"I thought you might be—" He stopped and shook his head. "It doesn't matter."

"Maybe I should make some introductions," the other man she'd mistaken for Lucian said, amused. "I'm Basilio, Lucian's brother."

Lucian kept his gaze on her. "It's rare to have an American working here." He shrugged. "But the economy is so bad, people get work where they can. Where are you staying?"

"Here," Nikki said.

"On the island?"

"Yes."

"Where?"

She gestured to the mansion. "At the house."

He rested a hand on his chest. "My house?"

"Yes."

He tilted his head to the side. "I thought I'd seen you before. There's something familiar about you. We must have met in passing?"

"No, but you met my sister, Monica Rozan."

His face split into a warm smile. "Yes, that's it. I see the resemblance."

"Few people do."

"Then they are blind."

Nikki blushed and looked away.

"What brings you to the island?"

Basilio broke in. "Why don't you get changed first, then talk?"

Nikki frowned. "I came because of you."

Lucian raised a dark eyebrow. "Me?"

Basilio shivered. "Don't you think it's gotten a little chilly? We should go inside."

Nikki ignored him. "Yes, to design a few rooms for you."

Lucian sent his brother a hooded glance. "Yes, the rooms," he said in an odd tone, the warmth in his gaze swiftly disappearing. "I'd forgotten about them. Let me change. Then we'll talk. Excuse me." He walked away.

Nikki felt her heart sinking as she watched him go. "He didn't know I was coming."

"No," Basilio said quickly, keeping his voice light. "As he said, he just forgot."

"He's not the type of man to forget anything. He didn't expect me to be here." She turned to Basilio. "What's going on?"

"Don't worry about it. He'll get used to the idea."

"So you're behind this?"

"Well, your sister thought—"

"My sister, too?"

"Nikki, please give this a chance. He needs your help. He just needs a little convincing, that's all. With you here, it will be a lot easier."

"I don't think so."

"Ready to go home?"

She knew it was a challenge—a dare. Was she brave enough to stay? Nikki thought about her office. Before she'd left New York, her office had been restored, she'd received a glowing report from the mistresses on their new place, she'd cleared her schedule for the next three months and she'd left Benjamin, who still expected a solid answer. No, she didn't want to go back to her old life. At least not just yet.

She drew her shoulders back and lifted her chin. "I want to stay. Let me show you how persuasive I can be."

Basilio smiled. "A woman after my own heart." He

took her elbow. "Come on. Let me walk you back to the house."

She turned and saw a black animal jump from one tree to another. She stepped back.

"Oh, don't mind him," Basilio said gently, nudging her forward. "That's just Lethe, Lucian's cat."

"Wasn't Lethe the river of forgetfulness in a myth?"

"Yes, that's my brother's strange sense of humor. There are many things he would like to forget."

Nikki glanced up at the golden eyes, which seemed to be following them.

"Don't worry. He rarely attacks."

Rarely didn't mean never. Nikki picked up her pace and changed the subject. "What did Callia mean when she was talking about ghosts?"

Basilio shook his head. "It's all her imagination. Pay no attention to her. She hasn't been the same since the fire. She sees things that aren't there. That's why Lucian hired Kay to stay with her."

Nikki nodded, not knowing what else to say. If it was all just Callia's imagination, why did Kay seem so on edge? But that wasn't her problem. She was here to redesign the house and nothing else.

As they approached the entrance, Nikki noticed a beautiful woman spreading a tablecloth on a wrought-iron glass table on the terrace. She looked like a lovely picture, but out of place. A sullenness surrounded her. She had a wild, elemental beauty, like the gathering of storm clouds that agitate the sea and make the leaves on the trees tremble.

"Who is that?" Nikki asked, intrigued by the woman.

"Iona. One of the few servants who stayed after the fire."

"Oh, she doesn't look happy."

Basilio shrugged. "It's work. Just stay out of her way and you'll be fine."

Nikki definitely would. The other woman looked up with liquid brown eyes. Nikki offered a smile, but the other woman didn't return it. It didn't matter, anyway. She had a more pressing issue.

She had to figure out how best to handle a man who didn't want to work with her. She had no one else to blame for the situation, since she hadn't let her sister explain anything and had run headlong into this project without getting all the details, such as was Lucian even interested? She knew that her sister and Lucian's brother had good intentions, but obviously there were reasons why Lucian didn't want the house redesigned. Were there still memories? Probably. But then again, after four years it was time for him to move forward and she could do that. She *would* do that. This was her golden opportunity and she wouldn't let him kick her out of paradise.

Chapter 4

"Get rid of her."

Basilio shut the door and watched his brother take a shirt from his closet. "Lucian, she just got here."

"Whose fault is that?"

"I was going to tell you about her."

Lucian buttoned up his shirt. "When?"

Basilio rubbed his chin. "When the time seemed right."

Lucian checked his reflection in the mirror. "Seems right now."

"She's really talented and—"

"I'm sure she's brilliant." He scowled at his reflection and unbuttoned his shirt. "I still don't want her here. Get rid of her." He tossed the shirt on the bed and grabbed another from the closet.

Basilio looked at his brother, helpless. "I can't just tell her to go."

"Fine. Pay her for her time."

Basilio sighed at his brother's tactlessness, then watched as Lucian straightened a sleeve. They had the same parents but were different in appearance due to the nearly ten-year age gap and their different skin tones from the mix of their European mother and African father. He'd gotten his mother's hair, and Lucian her eyes. He had their father's chin, while Lucian had his height. Basilio had only known his brother for less than a year before the fire. He'd sought him out after their mother's death. He had just finished college and wasn't sure what he wanted to do with his life yet, but one thing he did know was that he wanted to rebuild his relationship with his brother and start fresh.

It hadn't been easy, but he was beginning to understand him. He had watched him endure painful treatments and relearn simple tasks. Seeing Lucian's swift movements as he changed clothes filled him with pride and he knew each year his brother would get stronger, but something was different about him now. He wasn't himself; he seemed agitated and unsure. That wasn't like Lucian. He was always cool and certain.

Basilio started to smile. "She got to you."

Lucian adjusted his collar. "What?"

"What came over you out there? I've never seen you act that way."

"I don't know. I didn't expect…" He threw out his hand, annoyed. "Why was she dressed like an ordinary washerwoman?"

"Market woman."

"They look alike to me."

"She's a foreigner. She probably thought it was pretty or something."

"How like a woman to be deceitful," Lucian said, tossing another shirt aside.

"She didn't mean to deceive anyone. I know I should have told you about her sooner, but this is a good thing. I think she can help you."

"Help me?" Lucian's voice cracked in surprise. "I don't need help." He checked his reflection again.

"You've done the buttons wrong."

Lucian scowled. "I know that."

Basilio smiled, trying not to laugh. "She's really gotten you rattled."

"I'm not rattled."

Basilio glanced at the bed. "Then how come you've gone through four shirts? You don't usually care what you look like."

Lucian tucked in his shirt, then smoothed down his hair. "I just want to make a good impression. My first one was—"

"A shock?"

"Unfortunate," Lucian corrected.

"I don't think you can undo a first impression."

"I can try."

"I haven't seen you respond to a woman like that since—" He stopped, not wanting to bring up the past and Alana. "Not that I blame you. She's an attractive woman. I could imagine getting my leg over that."

"She's engaged. I saw the ring."

"Before or after you kissed her?"

Color swept into Lucian's cheeks. "I'll have to apologize about that. Perhaps I should send flowers to her room and add a diamond necklace."

"She'll see that as an insult."

"I thought women liked diamonds."

"That's not the point. You don't need to worry about the ring. It doesn't mean much."

"How do you know?"

"I know women, and the way you kissed her, I'm surprised she didn't slap you."

"It's only because she knew who I was. She was being polite."

"No, she wasn't being polite. She liked it."

Lucian's face lit up. "Really?" He held up his hand before his brother could respond. "Forget it. It doesn't matter. I don't care. I don't want her here. I've had enough trouble with designers, and things become more complicated when it comes to friends. Get rid of her."

"She likes you."

"Stop saying that."

"It's true."

"I'm not interested. She belongs to another man and I've learned my lesson. Most women can't be trusted. Especially ones who wear one man's ring and allow another to kiss them."

"Like you said, maybe she was just being polite."

Lucian frowned but didn't reply.

"Okay, aside from your first meeting, don't ignore this opportunity. You need to move on. Those empty rooms are a symbol of what happened. You need to think about the future."

"Why?"

"At least think about Callia."

"When I'm gone, she can design those rooms any way she wants."

"At least let Nikki try one room. It shouldn't take more than two weeks and then she'll be gone. Just two weeks and she'll be gone for good. No problem. We'll all get what we want."

"You think one room will take only two weeks?"

"I told you she's good. It may be even less." Basilio held out his hand. "Do we have a deal?"

Lucian sighed. "Fine. One room, then she goes."

Someone knocked.

"Come in," Lucian said.

Dante Andreas, Lucian's butler, entered. He sent Basilio a careless look, then focused on Lucian. Basilio didn't like him. He knew he was more than just a butler, but still wasn't sure of all his duties. He was only a few years older than Basilio, but seemed decades so. His nationality was Italian, but his appearance—tightly curled hair and dark skin—hinted at a heritage that spread far beyond those shores. At times Basilio envied the close bond he and Lucian had.

"I have Ms. Rozan waiting in the main room."

"Fine." Lucian looked at his brother. "Tell her I'll meet her there."

Basilio nodded. "Okay."

"And stop grinning. You haven't won yet."

"But I'm getting close," Basilio said, then strolled out of the room.

Dante closed the door once Basilio was gone. "She's an unexpected complication."

Lucian pounded his cane in exasperation. "Don't I know it."

"I'm sorry I wasn't aware of what your brother was up to."

"That's not your job. You're too busy with more important things."

"My job is to make sure this place is safe. He's causing trouble. I don't trust him. He just showed up out of nowhere and—"

"Not out of nowhere," Lucian carefully corrected. "And he isn't a stranger. He's family."

"Yes," Dante sighed. "But everything has gone bad since his arrival."

"Don't exaggerate. None of it is his fault, just a co-incidence."

"I don't like coincidences."

"Force yourself to like this one," Lucian said in an unrelenting tone.

Dante heard it and changed the subject. "You have two messages from France."

"They can wait."

"And Wanda called."

Lucian swore. "Keep her away from here."

Dante noticed the clothes on the bed and began to put them away. "I have. But I can't keep her away forever."

"Sure you can."

Dante smoothed out a shirt, then hung it up. "She'll just go to the press."

"Let her," Lucian said. He sat on his bed and put on his shoes. "Who'll listen?"

"If she drops your name, people will. You don't need that kind of publicity."

Lucian sighed. "You're right. I don't need another complication. What does she want?"

Dante closed the closet with a soft click. "You know what she wants."

"Fine. Schedule a time."

"When?"

"The sooner the better. Next month. I just want to get it over with."

"We'll have to tell Callia."

"Don't worry. I will. Thanks."

Dante nodded, then left the room. He walked outside and lit a cigarette. He had been Lucian's right hand for nearly seven years and had helped patrol the island for even longer than that. He knew about every coming and going. His reputation was stellar, except for one grievous stain—the fire at the Kontos mansion. He'd failed and nearly gotten his friend killed, as well as little Callia. He wouldn't rest until he uncovered the truth. He suspected it wouldn't be pretty. But he was used to ugly things. He'd grown up on the streets of Rome and London, before an aunt shipped him off to Greece, where he was put into an apprenticeship program with a bottling company. While it didn't pay very well, it provided Dante with the training, discipline and work ethic he would need later in life.

Dante took a long drag of his cigarette. He didn't like Basilio. He didn't trust a man who smiled so easily all the time. He had something to hide. How could he not have some envy for a brother whose success overshadowed his own? No, he didn't trust Basilio and would watch him.

Chapter 5

He still didn't know what had come over him. Lucian walked to the room where Nikki was waiting, searching his mind for an explanation. He hadn't been himself. All he knew was that after Nikki saved the kitten's life, he wanted to kiss her. He'd felt a mixture of lust, amazement and awe. She'd saved the kitten's life and made Callia happy. He'd wanted to feel that life force she'd given the kitten infuse him and make him feel whole and human again. Just one wild taste of those lips.

And she'd made him feel more than human. She'd made him feel like a god, and in a moment he knew he'd persuade her to be his lover. Whoever had laid claim to her be damned; they would have to fight him for her. He would make her his, using all the power and influence he had at his disposal.

But then he learned she wouldn't be an easy conquest. She wasn't some peasant woman here to work. She was J.D.'s sister-in-law. Off-limits to him. That changed everything. She didn't belong here. And he didn't like how she made him feel. He knew he'd agreed to let her stay two weeks, but there were other ways to break promises. He wanted her gone and he'd get his wish. He'd just have to make it look like it was her idea.

He'd been able to get rid of the other designers his brother had hired and she'd be no different. He'd be a bit more strategic, because he had to be careful with her. He didn't want to jeopardize his friendship with J.D. and Monica. He'd keep his distance, be cold like he'd been with the others, and she'd quit out of frustration. He knew his reputation and would use it to his advantage. Yes, he'd get her to quit. That shouldn't be too hard. Flash enough money in her face, be a jerk, and she'd be on the mainland by tomorrow.

Lucian walked into the room, expecting to see Nikki impatiently sitting and waiting for him. He'd deliberately made her wait an extra twenty minutes. Instead he saw her moving back and forth in the room like a butterfly flittering from one flower to another. She wasn't dressed in another market-woman outfit or in a chic, expensive suit, which one would expect a New York designer to wear, but in a patterned long skirt and top that reminded him of the plains of the Southwest. He half expected to hear the sound of horse hooves and smell the scent of wildflowers. He gripped his cane. Damn, now he was getting poetic. She was so full of light and energy, and she didn't belong here in this house. Dreams died here.

Nikki turned to him and frowned, then looked around the room again.

He guessed that she was trying to figure out from

the bare furniture what the room was for. "This room used to be—"

She shook her head. "I don't care what it *used* to be. What do you want it to be now?"

He walked over to a large leather couch off to the side and took a seat. Distance was essential. "The same thing. A welcoming room...area. Whatever..."

"Hmm." To his dismay Nikki sat down next to him, her perfume drifting toward him like a soft mist. He shifted, surprised by her actions. He thought Americans liked space.

"Let's get started."

"We already have," she said, pulling out a small suede portfolio she'd had resting on the side of the couch. "I've done some preliminary sketches based on the photos my sister showed me of some of your rooms." She spread them out on his lap. "Does any of this interest you?"

Lucian absently glanced over them. They were nice, but not memorable. "No."

Nikki gathered up the sketches, undisturbed by his abrupt response. "That's okay. It was just a start." She grabbed some color swatches and drapery material from inside the portfolio. "Have a look at these. Does anything strike you? Does a certain color stand out for you? Would you prefer paint or wallpaper?"

Lucian yawned, his gaze flat with evident boredom. "I don't care."

Nikki continued, determined not to be sidelined by his—disinterest. "Now, we haven't discussed a budget yet. If you—"

"Money is not a factor. If I like it, I'll pay for it."

"Okay. So do you want to go for extravagance or simple elegance?"

"Does it matter?"

"Of course it matters."

"What do you think?" he asked.

"It doesn't matter what I think. You're the client." She set her portfolio aside and clasped her hands together. "Since you don't want to look at any of these, let's just have a conversation. Tell me what this room means to you."

"Nothing."

"It must mean something."

Lucian looked around and shook his head. "No."

Nikki leaned closer. "Do you have *any* ideas you'd like to share?"

"No," he said, steeling himself against her bright gaze. He couldn't let her seep past his guard. He needed to let her know who was in charge. He held up his hand. "This is how it's going to work. You'll sketch three to five designs. I'll look them over, and if I like one, you're hired. If not, it was a pleasure to meet you." He stood. "Excuse me."

"Is that all you've got?"

He stopped and spun around. "What?"

Nikki stretched her arms nearly the length of the couch and crossed her legs. "Is that how you think you'll get rid of me? A few cold words and a dismissal?"

"I didn't say I wanted to get rid of you."

"You don't have to," she said, swinging her leg. "I know you don't want me here."

Lucian shrugged. There was no point in trying to deny it. "And yet you want to stay?"

"I like it here."

"It's early yet. I can make your stay very miserable."

Nikki shook her head. "You don't frighten me."

"That's because you're naive."

"No, it's because you gave me a chance to see another side of you. And no man who kisses the way you do can be completely ruthless. Close, but not completely. So as cold as you appear, I'll always know the truth."

"That kiss was a moment of weakness—"

"I'm glad to know you have them." She flashed a sly grin. "And what they are."

His tone hardened. "You don't want to tangle with me, Nikki. You'll lose."

"I'm stronger than I look."

"You bluff well."

"I'm not bluffing."

"No one enters this house without me knowing something about them."

"So?"

"So I know your weaknesses, too. You have more than a few."

"So what?" She shrugged. "I don't try to hide them."

Lucian walked over to her and rested one hand on the armrest and the other behind her. He knew it was risky to be this close to her, but he had to regain control of the situation.

"Really?" he said in a silky voice of challenge. "You don't try to hide that you're reckless? That you attended four different universities? That in the past two years you've lost six top clients to another firm, and the rumor has it that you only got your first job due to your sister's influence? Do you want the world to know that you originally wanted to be a painter but didn't have the talent, and no one bought your work, so you switched to fashion design, also failing miserably when even your sister, wearing your designs, couldn't garner any interest in your work, which is why you settled for interior design? You also nearly went bankrupt twice but had the right friends to help you out. And when it comes to men—"

"All right. Enough." Nikki's face paled, as if he'd slapped her. "You're right," she said, humbled, all light gone from her eyes. "You do play dirty." She stood and walked to the door.

Lucian swore. He hadn't meant to go that low. "I'll give you a week."

"I don't need your pity."

"Think of it as a compromise."

Nikki lowered her head but didn't turn. "How about twelve days?"

"Ten."

She spun around, her face spreading into a wide smile. "Okay."

Lucian stared at her, thunderstruck. All paleness had left her face; she glowed with triumph. "Wait. You—" He pointed at her. "That was all an act?"

She sauntered over to him. "I told you I'm stronger than you think." She stopped a foot away from him. "Feel like kissing me again?"

Yes, and a lot more. He tapped the head of his cane. "I feel like strangling you."

She winked. "That's fine." She trailed a finger along his jaw. "I'm into that, too."

He grabbed her hand, but it didn't stop the memory of her searing touch. This was all wrong. She was supposed to be afraid of him. He had to get control of this situation. He glanced at her ring. "What's his name?"

She paused. "Who?"

He lifted her hand. "Your fiancé."

Nikki looked down at her hand with a bored expression and wiggled her fingers. "Benjamin." She let her hand fall. "And he's not my fiancé yet. He asked, and at first I said yes, then changed my mind."

"Do you do that a lot?"

"No, I'm trying to learn not to be reckless, as you call it. I told him I had to think about it. I haven't given him an answer yet."

"So you wear his ring to torment him?"

"No, he asked me to. He wanted me to think of him."

"I think your memory is fading."

"Probably."

Lucian shook his head. "Benjamin may be a fool, but I'm not. Design the room and that's it." He turned.

"You still haven't told me what you want." She rested a hand on her hip. "Even though I can probably guess."

"Yes, take a wild guess. I always get what I want." He threw a cold smile over his shoulder. "The question is, will you be the woman to give it to me?"

Chapter 6

The moment he was gone, Nikki collapsed in a chair and shut her eyes. She'd won round one, and it had been harder than she'd thought, because in truth he did frighten her. Not in a terrifying way, but in an elemental way. It was as if he really could strip her bare and see all her faults and weaknesses and turn them against her. He'd come close by mentioning her past. The fact that her sister had helped her get her first client was still somewhat of a sore spot. Her beautiful sister always got credit when things went well. Nikki didn't.

She'd been born during the coldest winter, on the longest night of the year. A night so long, some feared the moon had replaced the sun.

Growing up, her sister had been kept inside, looked after by various instructors and attendants, while Nikki had been free to roam. Her parents had loved her but had never really given her much notice. She was always in her sister's shadow. But everyone near Monica Dupree was cast in her shadow. Thankfully, her kind disposition made you feel welcome in her presence, instead of in competition. So Nikki couldn't dislike her sister—instead she felt a sense of pride—but their different lives kept them apart. They had lived in the same house growing up but hadn't shared the same meals, because Monica had a "special" diet that was created to maintain the healthy glow of her skin and hair, while keeping her weight down. Even as they aged, they never went clothes shopping together or to the park or the beach. Monica was treated like a rare heirloom—treasured and guarded.

When Monica met, then married Delong, the distance between them grew wider. The year of silence after Delong's death still haunted Nikki. She felt guilty that she hadn't tried harder to rebuild their relationship. Perhaps she would have discovered the danger her sister had been in. She might have tried more to find her. Had part of her been glad that her sister had disappeared from her life? That for a moment she could shine?

In a way she was still in her sister's shadow, because she wouldn't have gotten this assignment without her sister's help, and Lucian knew it. He hadn't chosen her; he was tolerating her. Once again she was just Monica's little sister. But she wouldn't let pride stand in the way. How she got there didn't matter. She would prove that she had her own light. That she was her own woman. She'd made a lot of mistakes in her past, but this project wouldn't be one of them.

Nikki would make sure that Lucian knew that. Lucian. She still couldn't form a complete opinion of him, but she knew one thing: She wanted him to kiss her again, just to make sure that the feel of his lips on hers had been real and not a dream. That the feelings he'd evoked in her hadn't been her imagination. The cool tycoon who'd just left her seemed nothing like the man she'd met outside: a man with a wet shirt clinging to a muscular chest and strong, impressive arms. He must have worked hard to regain that kind of strength. For a moment she thought of Lucian as the god Hades, king of the underworld and the wealth hidden in the earth, and with his kiss she'd become Persephone, queen of the underworld, his dark hunger becoming hers.

But her fantasy was short-lived. Once he'd known who she really was, all interest disappeared and he'd ripped away any possibility of a tie between them, and just as quickly that god was replaced by a man in an austere gray shirt and dark trousers. Lucian looked like his reputation, but Nikki couldn't forget that just for a moment she'd met a man who smelled of the sea and the earth, whose lips were both salty and sweet, and how weightless she'd felt in the circle of his arms. She wanted to unmask that man again. With her eyes still closed, Nikki removed Benjamin's ring and slipped it into her pocket. It wasn't fair to him to feel this way about another man.

Nikki sighed and opened her eyes and saw a piece of patterned cloth lying against the wall. She walked over and picked it up. It was a beautiful embroidered West African cloth usually used as a head wrap. Why would someone have left it on the floor?

Nikki shrugged and went over to a mirror to try it on. She expertly tied it, remembering an aunt who used to wear her hair this way. Once finished, she smiled at her reflection. It didn't look like the typical designs one would see an ordinary woman wear. The thin, almost invisible gold thread was not the work of a casual tailor. Wearing the cloth made her feel regal.

"So how long do you have?" a voice said from behind.

Nikki spun around, startled, but Callia seemed equally startled as she stared back at the head wrap Nikki wore. "Where did you get that?" she asked, coming up to her, absently stroking Pauline, who was cradled in her arms, as she did so.

Nikki was surprised to see her alone, considering what Basilio had told her. "Where's Kay?"

Callia shrugged, looking a little mischievous, as if she'd gotten away with something she shouldn't have. "So where did you get it?" she asked again.

"I just saw it lying on the floor." Nikki stared at her reflection again. "It's beautiful," she said, touching the patterned cloth. "I'm guessing West African."

"Ghanaian." Callia walked up behind her and also stared at her reflection. "I've traveled there twice, but—" She stopped. "Do you have African blood?"

"My father's people hailed from Togo many years ago."

"That must be it," Callia said in an odd tone.

Nikki opened her mouth to ask her what she meant, but Callia spun away and sat down on the nearby couch. Like her uncle Lucian, something about her had also changed. Inside the house she seemed older, not as whimsical as she'd been outside. She didn't appear like a young woman who'd talk about ghosts, and there were shadows in her eyes. Instead she looked like a privileged teenager in an expensive summer dress, with an attractiveness she didn't know how to use to her advantage. At least not yet.

"So how long will you stay?"

"Ten days."

"That's more than most." Callia pointed to a corner. "There used to be a piano there and a harp. She liked to play the harp. She could play beautifully. Sometimes I still think I hear her play."

"Who?"

"Alana. Uncle was going to marry her."

"What happened? Where is she?"

"She's dead," Callia said in a bored, matter-of-fact tone. "The walls were cream and there were…"

Nikki didn't listen to the rest. Lucian had wanted to marry a woman who died? Was that part of the feeling of tragedy and sadness that gripped the house? Suddenly, Nikki knew she couldn't work with the past; she had to deal with the present. And in order to do so, she had to know more about him.

Nikki removed the head wrap and set it aside. "Can you tell me a little more about your uncle?"

Callia hesitated. "He's a very private person."

Nikki smiled. "I don't need dark secrets. Does he have any hobbies?"

Callia looked up at her with a blank expression.

"Things that he enjoys," Nikki added, clarifying her question.

"He likes to swim at night down at the beach, near the cove. Alone."

Nikki waited. "And?"

"And what?"

Nikki sighed, realizing that was all the young woman was willing to reveal. Perhaps if she got to know her more, she would trust her. Nikki sat down next to her. "Pauline is a beautiful kitten." She looked much better and Nikki could see her fluffy orange-colored fur.

"Thanks for saving her. Do you have pets?"

"No, but my sister has a dog."

"Dogs are nice, but I prefer cats."

"Do you like living here?"

"Not anymore."

Nikki stared at Callia, surprised. "Then why do you stay? You could convince your uncle to let you stay at his other house, or I'm sure you could go to a boarding school or…"

Callia shook her head. "Uncle doesn't want to be anywhere else right now and I don't want to leave Uncle Lucian here alone. Someone has to look out for him." She glanced around the room and lowered her voice to a whisper. "The ghost will get him. She wants him dead."

Nikki knew the fire had been from arson, but couldn't understand Callia's fear of a ghost. "Are they still looking for the arsonist?"

"No. We know who did it. We just don't know how."

"Then that person has been arrested, right?" Nikki said, wondering if she should start looking for Kay. Was Callia on any medication to keep her from these delusions? But then again there was a sense of sanity about her. But ghosts didn't kill, even if one did believe in them. "Your uncle's safe now."

"No, she still haunts the place and will get her revenge."

"Who?"

"Alana."

"Why?"

"Callia!" a deep voice said.

Callia jumped like a scared child and turned to the door, where Lucian stood in the hallway. "Yes, Uncle Lucian?"

"Kay's been frantically looking for you. Come here."

Nikki held up her hand. "As you can see, she's safe here with me. Kay can join us if she wants to, but we're having an important conversation right now. You can talk to her when I'm finished."

"I want to talk to her now."

Nikki smiled. "Then you're going to be disappointed." She pointed at him. "Say one more word and my ten days start tomorrow."

Lucian narrowed his eyes but didn't reply and left.

"Now, what were you saying?" Nikki said, annoyed by Lucian's interruption at such a key point.

Callia stared at her, wide-eyed.

"What?" Nikki wiped her cheek. "Is there something on my face?"

Callia slowly sank back into her seat. "No one has ever spoken to Uncle Lucian like that. I'm surprised he didn't fire you."

"He's thinking about it, I'm sure," Nikki said in a dry tone.

Callia tilted her head and studied the woman sitting beside her. "You're different. You're not afraid of him. Most people are—especially women."

Basilio strolled in with his hands in his pockets. "What the hell just happened? Lucian's laughing his head off."

"Really?" Callia said, amazed. "I wish I could have seen that."

"He wouldn't tell me why, though."

Callia gestured to Nikki. "It's because of her."

Basilio looked at Nikki with admiration. "How did you manage that?"

"I didn't do it on purpose," Nikki said, unwilling to take credit.

"You should have seen the way she spoke to him, like he was a servant," Callia said, then imitated Nikki's response to Lucian's request.

Basilio burst into laughter.

Nikki shook her head, ashamed. "I wasn't that bad."

Callia lifted her nose and took on an affected tone. "If you say one more word, my ten days start tomorrow."

Basilio laughed harder.

Nikki couldn't help a grin. She'd been around the Seventh Avenue crowd too long. "I just lost my temper."

"He has that effect on people," Basilio said.

"And how do people respond to you?" Nikki asked.

He rested a hand on his chest with false modesty. "People love me."

"When you're gone," Callia added.

"Be quiet, little girl."

Callia made a face.

Basilio gently yanked her from the couch and took her place next to Nikki.

"Hey!" Callia cried.

He rested his arm along the back of the couch and ignored her. He grinned at Nikki. "How would you like to go out on the yacht tomorrow?"

"I'm not on vacation," Nikki said, unsure if he was flirting or making a pass. Either way she was enjoying the attention.

"You can work if you want to, but I doubt you will," he told her.

"It's lovely being on the water," Callia said.

Basilio sent her a look. "Who said you're invited?"

"I'm coming, anyway."

Before he could argue, Nikki said, "I'd love to."

He winked. "I'll see you then," he said and left.

"You'd better go and find out what your uncle wants," Nikki said.

Callia sighed, unwilling to leave. "He wants to give me a lecture for escaping from Kay's watchful eyes."

"Perhaps if you behave, he'll discover that you don't need her anymore."

"Maybe." Callia walked to the door, then stopped and turned. "Who do you like more? Basilio or Uncle Lucian?"

"I hardly know them yet," Nikki said, surprised by the question. "I don't know."

"I do," Callia said in a singsongy voice, then walked away.

Nikki sat back on the couch and sank into deep thought. Here was a strange young girl caught between girlhood and womanhood, living with two very different brothers. It was an odd household. One brother was handsome and refined, while the other one was rugged and rough. Nikki looked down at her bare hand with a stab of guilt, but knowing it was the right choice. She wasn't ready to settle down yet and her life in New York was beginning to feel far away in more ways than one.

Once he left the room, Basilio let his smile drop. Two weeks wasn't enough time. He'd have to do more to convince his brother to let Nikki stay. She was the key.

"You shouldn't frown like that," the maid, Iona, said, meeting him in the hall. "It makes you look fierce like your brother."

"I don't care."

She grabbed his arm and pulled him into the conservatory.

"What are you doing?" he asked as Iona slid her arm around his neck.

She brushed her lips against his. "You have ignored me all day."

He anxiously looked around. "I have to be careful."

"How long will she stay?"

"Only a couple weeks, but I'll work on it. She's good for him."

"Yes," Iona said, kissing him again. "Your brother needs something to keep him occupied so he'll leave you alone."

"He already does."

"Not often enough. He babies you and tells you what to do."

"Big brothers are like that sometimes," Basilio said, feeling the need to defend Lucian. He had been there after the death of their mother and had paid for his schooling. At first he'd meant only to visit Lucian on the island to relax and figure out his life. Then he decided to stay and help manage the rental of several villas Lucian had constructed throughout the island and the exclusive guests allowed to visit or rent them. He wasn't ambitious. He liked the easy life. Iona had been a surprise. He'd never met a woman like her before.

Like any man, he'd noticed her immediately, but never thought to pursue anything. It was the tragedy of the fire that had brought them close. She'd bolstered him up when he feared his brother wouldn't make it through all his surgeries. But most of all she'd assuaged his guilt about losing track of Callia. He'd been careless, and though his brother didn't blame him, he could feel his brother's disappointment. But Iona didn't judge him. She understood that he'd just made a mistake that night. He'd gone drinking and thought Callia was safe.

Iona had helped him to get over that awful night. There were so many things he didn't remember that she helped him to accept or that she convinced him to forget. She was an older woman who made him feel like a man. He knew his relationship with her was risky, but he couldn't help himself. She was his salvation. Plus, he liked how she pressed her full body against him.

She nibbled his earlobe. "I want you to follow *my* orders."

"Don't I most times?" he responded, his breathing becoming more rapid with her body pressed close to his.

Iona suddenly drew away, leaving him aching for more. She did that to him a lot. "Shh, I hear footsteps." She fixed her hair and he adjusted his shirt.

Lucian entered moments later and found Basilio standing near the window, while Iona pretended to polish a vase. "Iona, you're wanted in the kitchen," he said.

She nodded, then left.

"I'd better get going, too," Basilio said.

Lucian blocked his path. "Stay away from that trouble."

"What?"

"You heard me clearly."

Basilio folded his arms and leaned against the wall. "She's not a thing. She's a woman."

"And you're a man and she's using that fact to her advantage. She's no good for you. As I said, she's trouble."

"Because she's part of your house staff?"

"That's only one reason. She's here because she's a good long-term worker and isn't superstitious about

this place. If you want to mess with staff, find someone else's."

"But you choose the best," he teased.

Lucian found no humor in his brother's remark. He
lifted his shirt sleeve, baring his scars. "Let me be a
lesson to you. Don't be fooled by a pretty face and a
soft body. She doesn't see you. She sees a ticket out.
A target. She'll use your heart against you and come
between us. Don't let that happen. Stay away, little
brother."

"Not every woman is like Alana."

Lucian rolled down his sleeve. "I know." He met his
brother's gaze. "Some are worse."

Kay hated having to take the mysterious phone calls
by the cove at night, but her contact gave her no choice.
She stood and heard a motorboat that went back and
forth between the mainland and the island, and then she
heard the call of a night bird. When her phone rang, she
jumped, then answered and heard the disguised voice
on the other end.

"The designer's staying ten days," the voice said.

"I know. I heard."

"But she may not last that long."

"She's not like the rest."

"That's good. She may be useful to us. Did you do
as I asked you?"

"Yes, but don't you think it's risky with another
person here?"

"No, it's even better."

"But if she sees me—"

"Make sure she doesn't."

"I'm always careful, but with another person around,
it could make things complicated."

"Not if you do what you're told. Having her here will make things harder for Kontos. He can't keep track of everything and this designer is perfect. Have you looked at her?"

"Yes. I just don't think—"

"I'm the one who thinks, not you. Don't back out on me and don't disappoint me."

Chapter 7

A piercing scream shot through Nikki's pleasant dream that night and startled her awake. She blinked in the darkness, then reached for her lamp. Bright light flooded the room, eradicating the darkness, but the screams continued. She grabbed a robe and rushed into the hallway, nearly knocking over Kay.

"What's happening?" she asked as the other woman rushed down the hall.

"It's just Callia."

Nikki followed Kay into Callia's bedroom and saw the young woman twisting and turning in a bed so large, she appeared as small as a six-year-old child. She moved as if her bedsheets were trying to strangle her. Her face was wet with sweat; her eyes squeezed shut as though she were in mental anguish. Kay stood next to the bed and raised her hand to slap her.

Nikki grabbed her arm. "Don't you dare do that."

Kay looked at Nikki, anxious and confused. "I always do it this way. It will help her get out of her nightmare."

Nikki looked at her with disgust. "There's another way to do it. A kinder, less violent way."

Kay yanked her arm away. "Let me do my job! I know her better than you do."

Nikki shoved her aside. "I will not let you slap this child."

"He's dead!" Callia screamed. "She killed him."

"You're letting her suffer," Kay said, waving her hands.

Nikki took one of Callia's shoulders. "He's all right, Callia. He's right here."

"She's come to kill him," she said, tears escaping from under her eyelids. "Now he's dead and I saw her!"

"No, he's safe in bed. Just like you. You're safe." Nikki shook Callia awake. "Open your eyes. It's all a dream."

Callia's eyes slowly fluttered open, but Nikki knew she wasn't with them. She kept her voice calm. "He's safe."

"He's safe? But I saw her here. She was standing in the main room with me, wearing the—" Callia shook her head. "She's come back and the fire—"

"She's still in a dream state," Kay interrupted, clearly annoyed and angry. "You're not helping."

"Leave her to me," Nikki snapped.

"Mr. Kontos won't like this."

"Well, he's not here to complain right now, so be quiet."

"The child is mad. She lost her mind that night."

Nikki glared at her. "And I'll lose my temper if you don't stop talking."

Kay folded her arms.

"She's still here in the house," Callia said. "I see her roaming the halls. I smell her when I sleep and the music plays."

"There's no music playing. It's just us." Nikki stroked Callia's forehead. "Everyone is safe. Callia, wake up."

Slowly realization descended and Callia became awake. She stared at Nikki for a long moment, then said, "Did I cry out?"

"Yes."

"What did I say?"

"Nothing," Kay said.

"You were talking about Alana," Nikki told her.

"Oh, yes…she's here. I can feel that she's here and I think I see her."

"But you know that's impossible," Kay said.

Nikki patted Callia's leg. "No one is here but us."

"I'm so afraid," Callia said in a small voice.

"Then I'll be strong for you. I won't leave until you fall back asleep," Nikki promised.

Callia's eyes filled with tears. Then she collapsed in Nikki's arms. "People think I'm crazy, but I'm not."

"I know you're not," Nikki said in a soothing voice. "You just sense things people don't see."

Callia raised her head and nodded. "Yes, that's right. That night, when we flew to the mainland, I knew something was wrong and I told Basilio, but he just ignored me, as always. I'd wished I could be with Uncle Lucian and then suddenly I was. I don't know how I got back here. I don't remember much else about that night, just that she was there and she was evil. And people think she's gone because she died in the fire. But she's still here."

Nikki didn't quite know what to say. Was the child crazy? What could account for the blank parts of her memory and her colorful imagination? She gently touched the girl's cheek. "You will keep him safe. Don't be fearful. Your gift will come in handy one day."

"You think it's a gift, not a curse?"

Nikki wasn't sure what it was. "No, you're not cursed."

"How do you know?"

Nikki hesitated, wondering how much to reveal. Should she tell her about the women in her family? About the one who used herbs to both kill and heal and another who could see spirits in the wind and read stones? "Let's just say that the women in my family have special gifts."

"What's your gift?"

"Helping young girls go back to sleep."

"The dark doesn't frighten you?"

"No." Nikki bit her lip. "Sometimes darkness can be beautiful."

Callia hugged her. "I'm so glad you're here. You understand me. No one else does."

"Yes," Nikki said in a low voice and looked over at Kay. "We're fine now. You can go get some rest."

Kay gave a terse nod, then left the room.

Sensing the mood shift, Pauline crept out from under the bed and brushed up against Nikki's leg. Nikki picked the kitten up and placed her on Callia's lap.

"See, nothing to fear," she said as Pauline began to purr.

"You'll stay longer than ten days," Callia said with certainty.

"I haven't even begun yet."

"But you will stay longer. I know you will. This

house needs you." Callia leaned against the headboard. "For the first time I feel okay. Almost happy."

"Good. That's because we're going on the yacht tomorrow. Now, get under the covers. You have to sleep so that you'll be rested for our journey." Nikki stood and straightened the bedclothes as Callia slipped down into them.

Callia looked up at her. "I'm really glad you're here."

"Me too." She tucked in the sheets, then sat in a soft armchair over by the window. "Sleep tight," she said, then waited for Callia's even breathing before she tiptoed out of the room and gently closed the door.

In the hallway the sleek, dark figure of the cat, Lethe, strolled past her, giving her goose bumps as his golden eyes briefly regarded her. He brushed up against her leg. She remained still, not bending to pet him. She wasn't suspicious about black cats, but this one made her uneasy.

"I'm just going to my room," she told the cat.

"Ah, I see Artemis is at work again," Lucian said, referring to the goddess he'd compared Nikki to at their first meeting. He'd appeared as if out of nowhere, but surprisingly his presence did not startle or frighten her.

Nikki rushed to explain. "I was just—"

"Come. Let's have a drink." Lucian turned, not giving her a chance to refuse him, not that she would have.

Nikki followed him outside to the terrace, where a collection of colorful candles sat on the table, providing small flickers of light against the still dark night. The stars hung high in the sky—bright, but distant, like the cold smile of a beautiful woman.

The heady scent of blossoms enveloped her in their fragrance, as if they'd been waiting for the day to end before revealing themselves. Nikki sat back on the wrought-iron chair and accepted the cool dry wine Lucian poured and sliced cheese. He'd been expecting her. For what she wasn't sure. She took a sip of the wine, then stared at him, unsure of his silence.

"About this afternoon—"

"It's the past," Lucian said with a dismissive wave of his hand. He rested his chin in his hand and studied her, the flame of one of the candles dancing in his emerald eyes. "I wanted to thank you for what you did tonight. I've never seen anyone handle Callia the way you did. How did you know what to do?"

Nikki hesitated at first, not sure how to accept his praise. She hadn't been aware that he had been there, watching her. "I know a little something about nightmares."

He paused. "Really?"

"Yes," she said in a curt tone, not wanting to elaborate. He knew too much about her already.

He sighed. "Me, too."

"Do you have nightmares about the fire?"

He lowered his gaze. "About a lot of things," he said in a bleak tone, "but I'm worried about Callia."

"My sister told me that she's not your daughter. She's your ward, someone you take care of."

"Yes, she was the daughter of my best friend. We were friends and business partners. I had a major business deal I had to take care of in Spain, but then something else came up and he took my place. The plane he was traveling on crashed into the ocean. A plane that I should have been on. I blamed myself, as did his widow, Wanda, who thought that I was the reason, she felt, he loved our business more than his family. I offered to look after her and the child. She just handed Callia over to me. She was only two at the time. Wanda told me she wanted me to always remember and feel guilty about what I'd stolen from her. The guilt aspect didn't work. Callia has made me feel as if a part of my friend is still alive. And I'm grateful for that.

"His widow became a bitter woman who drinks. One night she ran her car off the road and right into a tree. She survived the accident with a broken back. She regained the use of her upper body but can't walk. She still lives in the family home with round-the-clock care. She won't let me adopt Callia and has Callia visit her four times a year. When she does, Wanda tries to poison her against me. When she was old enough, I told Callia how her father died and why she ended up living with me. She doesn't seem to care about what happened. Instead, every year our bond appears to grow stronger."

"Why would she care? Her father's death wasn't your fault."

"I'm a lucky man when it comes to making money, but that's about it." Lucian looked out at the dark expanse of the sea.

Nikki sipped her wine, then stared at it. "I know what you mean."

Lucian raised his brows, surprised. "Do you?"

"Yes. My life hasn't been as charmed as my sister's, although she has had her share of tragedy and heartbreak. Nothing has ever come easily to me. Everything has been work. Some are born with luck and the rest of us have to create it. But I don't think we're just victims of fate."

"Hmm," Lucian said, then fell silent again.

"I'm going on the yacht tomorrow with Basilio and Callia. Would you like to join us?" Nikki said, trying to lighten the mood.

Lucian lifted his glass, his steady laughing gaze meeting hers across the rim. "And spoil my brother's fun? No."

"Your brother is too young for me."

He set his glass down. "And I'm too old."

"I don't think so."

Lucian stood and took a bloom from the garden and bent it toward Nikki, allowing its sweet scent to reach her. "How many men worship at your altar?" he asked in a deep tone.

"Not many."

He let the petals of the flower brush her cheek. "I don't believe you."

"They don't."

"Are you telling me that no man has ever told you that he would gather all the stars in the heavens to wrap around your neck?" Lucian said in a smooth, velvet voice. "Or sweep the depths of the sea to uncover all its treasures to lay at your feet, and collect the rarest silkworms to adorn you in the finest garments ever created if you granted him your devotion?"

Nikki swallowed, her entire body filled with wanting. "No," she said, breathless. "No man has ever said that."

The flower in his hand brushed her neck. "Just Benjamin."

Her skin tingled at the touch. "He doesn't worship me."

Lucian touched the flower against her mouth. "I bet you just don't notice, because you think that kind of interest belongs only to your sister. But, Nikki, there are men who prefer the moonlight to the sun."

She searched his face. "Why are you saying these things?"

"I thought you knew what I wanted."

Nikki licked her lips. Yes, she did, but she didn't expect this. "I do."

"You've bewitched me. You sit there, quietly watching me with those eyes of yours, unafraid, but also unsure. I can see a cascade of emotions crossing your face, but I can't read them. You intrigue me, even when I don't want you to. I can't afford to. But it feels good because you make me forget...." He gripped his hand into a fist. "You make me forget things I have no right to." He brushed the flower against the hollow of her neck, his gaze trailing behind it like a slow, sensual caress. "Perhaps I'm wrong. You're not a goddess. You're a sorceress."

"No," Nikki said, breathless and tense lest she do or say anything to break the invisible bond between them. "I have no magic in me."

"That I find hard to believe."

Lucian lifted Nikki to her feet and his mouth covered hers. The touch and taste of his lips were even better than she remembered. Her entire body came alive at his touch. The air felt more fragrant, the breeze cooler and his body solid and as hot as volcanic fire. She surrendered to the demanding mastery of his hands and the practiced persuasion of his mouth. Every fiber of her body went weak at his touch.

He pulled away, his eyes smoldering with fire, but his voice cool. "I didn't expect this."

"Neither did I."

"I shouldn't let this happen."

"Then blame me," Nikki said, bold and impulsive. She wrapped her arms around his neck and kissed him.

"Are you sure?"

"Yes."

"Can I blame you for this?" Lucian asked as he untied her robe and pushed it from her shoulders. "And this?" He removed a strap from her nightie and slid it down until he captured one breast in his hand. "And this?" His mouth covered her breast, his tongue warm and wet against her taut nipple.

Nikki closed her eyes, her hands diving into his hair, wanting his tongue to explore every part of her. "Yes, blame me for everything."

"I want to," Lucian said, now letting his mouth slide down her throat. "But I can't."

"You can try."

He lifted his face and offered her an indulgent smile. "Then what kind of man would that make me?"

"A man under a spell."

He paused and Nikki felt the magic moment shatter. "Yes." He drew away and a shadow fell over his eyes as he looked at her. "I was under a spell once by a sorceress who turned me into a beast." He lifted up the strap of her nightie until she was fully clothed again. "I've learned my lesson."

Nikki grabbed his arm before he could turn from her. "One woman may have turned you into a beast, but let another turn you back into a man."

A cynical grin touched his lips. "At what price?"

"No price."

"There's always a price."

"We can figure that out later." She tugged on his sleeve. "Let me see your scars."

"Why? They are the stuff of nightmares."

"I told you before that I'm used to nightmares."

He removed his shirt. "Even living ones?" He turned his back to her.

Nikki recoiled at the hideous sight where dark,

gnarled flesh met raw red and black skin. The scars covered his entire back and one arm. She bit back a gasp she didn't want him to hear.

But he heard it, anyway, and quickly turned to her, his scarred arm reaching for her. She flinched just for a moment but it was enough. A faint light died in his eyes and his hand fell. He grabbed his shirt.

Nikki silently swore, guilt piercing through her like a shard of glass. "Lucian, I didn't mean—"

"To recoil from my touch?" he said in a harsh voice. "How could you stop yourself?"

Nikki shook her head, her body trembling as her mind desperately searched for the right words to repair the damage she'd done. "Lucian, please. It wasn't you. I just didn't—"

"Don't pity me, damn you." He ground the words out between his teeth. "And don't look at me like that! Like some wounded creature that needs to be soothed and coddled. Or like a child that needs to be rocked back to sleep after a bad dream. This is my reality, Nikki, and there's no way to disguise it or pretty it up." He picked up his drink and emptied its contents in one swallow, then slammed the glass down with such force, she was surprised it didn't crack. "Good night." He grabbed his cane and stormed away.

Nikki fell back into her chair as the weight of her misery descended on her, tightening her throat. She blew out the candles and in the darkness let her tears fall.

Chapter 8

Light danced along the blue water as Nikki lay on the sundeck of the yacht. She was glad for the bright sun, which gave her an excuse to wear the sunglasses that hid her red-rimmed eyes. She'd hardly slept last night, wishing she'd handled everything differently. Why had she flinched? She'd had his trust and lost it in an instant. It wasn't that his scars had frightened or disgusted her, just that they still looked so painful, and she could feel the agony he must have been in. If only he'd allowed her to explain. But she still couldn't deny that she'd handled it badly.

Monica wouldn't have flinched. She would have steeled herself and made him feel like a king. Instead, she'd made him feel like a monster. How could she have regained his trust at that moment? She could have told him about her recurring nightmare that someone she loved was in danger and she was unable to save them.

That she was always too late or they were just out of reach. At first those dreams featured just Monica. Then, when her niece, Starla, was born, she started showing up in her dreams, crying, with her arms outstretched to her aunty—begging for help she couldn't give. Now even little Markos appeared in her dreams, and just like with the others, she was always too late and failed to help him. Like Callia, sometimes she woke up at night in tears, knowing that she'd awakened from a nightmare about her deepest fear, but still feeling like a failure. But she wasn't sure if telling Lucian about her dreams and fears would have changed the hurt she'd caused him.

She'd failed him just as much as if he had been swept out to sea and had thrown a rope for her to catch. She'd missed and let it slip through her grasp, letting him drown. It was like a real-life version of her nightmare coming true. Would she always fail the people she cared for? At that moment she knew what she had to do. She would have to make up for her involuntary action through her work. She would design a spectacular room for him.

"You're lost in thought," Basilio said, setting his glass aside.

"Who can think in paradise?" Nikki said, not wanting to share her thoughts.

"Yes, you're right. I find it hard myself sometimes."

"That explains a lot," Callia said, stretched out in the lounge chair next to Nikki.

He ignored her and pointed to several spots of land in the distance. "That's Greece and over there's Turkey."

Nikki glanced at them, then looked back at Lucian's island—remote and beautiful with its hidden secrets.

Basilio noticed her look. "It used to be called Smugglers' Island. The name changed but the activity hasn't."

Nikki turned to him, stunned. "People still smuggle from here? What are you doing about it?"

"We leave it to the patrol. You don't have to be worried. Lucian's hired the best and none of our visitors have ever complained. But be careful going around at night, especially when you're near the water. We have lots of security, but it's still a large island and you could get lost."

A large island with few visitors, Nikki thought. But one woman had made an impact on its owner. "Tell me about Alana."

Callia and Basilio stilled, thickening the silence in the air, until Basilio said, "Why?"

"Callia told me that Lucian was going to marry her and that she died."

He shot Callia a glance.

"It's true," the girl said.

He shrugged. "Yes, but it wasn't as straightforward as that."

"How do you mean?" Nikki asked.

He sighed, uncomfortable. "I suppose you'll find out eventually. Alana started the fire and then perished in it."

Nikki stared at him, horrified. "Why would she do such a thing?"

"Because she's evil," Callia said.

"No, it's not that simple," Basilio said. "Before you can understand, let me give you some background." He settled back into his lounge chair, as if part of him enjoyed the job of sharing the story. "Alana was the daughter of a top Ghanaian official he met in Switzerland. The moment he saw her, Lucian fell in love, but he didn't know she had a dark side. She could be moody, temperamental and nasty to the servants and anyone who crossed her. Or who she *thought* crossed her. When Lucian discovered this and some other things about her, he broke off the engagement. So she got her revenge by setting the place on fire."

Nikki shook her head. "That seems like a rather extreme action just for getting dumped."

"I know, but if you'd met Alana, you'd know that is exactly something she would do."

"There must have been more to the story for her to be so violently angry."

"If there is, only Lucian knows. Alana liked drama. Some believe she poured accelerant around the house, then on herself, and torched both while Lucian watched. Others think she meant to burn only the house down and got caught in her own trap. Stories and rumors linger, but only Lucian knows the truth and he won't discuss it with anyone. All we know is that her body was found, broken and charred, at the side of the house." He sent Callia a hooded look. "One thing is certain. She's definitely dead."

"But it seems so vicious. Was she crazy?"

"I didn't think so. I don't think anyone did, but she must have been and we just discovered it too late."

Callia shook her head. "She wasn't crazy and she isn't done yet."

"I don't believe in ghosts," Basilio said.

"That doesn't mean it's not real," Callia countered. "She's a—"

"The only mystery," Basilio interrupted, "was how she got into the house."

Nikki leaned forward. "You think someone on the staff might have helped her?"

"There's no other way. The security system is stellar. The way she was able to make the place go up in flames took skill and cunning. She knew the layout of the entire house and had to have the time to set things up for the house to explode the way it did. Someone hid her and helped her into the house."

"You think someone else wanted revenge?"

"No, I think Alana used someone who didn't know what she was really planning to do. After the fire most of the staff left and those who returned have been loyal for years. We can vouch for everyone. I'm sure whoever helped her is long gone."

"You say she was Ghanaian?" Nikki asked.

"Yes. Why?"

"Yesterday I found a beautiful head wrap in one of the rooms I was in." Nikki described it for him.

"Yes," Callia said, excited. "I saw it too. It looked just like the family colors."

Basilio frowned. "That's strange."

"Family colors?" Nikki said, picking up on Callia's words.

"Our father was from a royal family in Ghana and that particular pattern you described represents our lineage, but after he disappeared nearly twenty years ago, we haven't had much to do with that side of the family," Basilio explained. "I think that's why Alana was able to captivate Lucian so much. Deep inside he was still desperate to connect to that part of his heritage. I think she used that against him."

"Have you been to Ghana?"

"Once," Basilio said with a careless twist of his wrist. "Lucian's several years older than me, so he remembers it and our father more than I do. We never lived there but I remember one visit we took to see

family. I admit I'm not that interested in going back.
Our parents met as university students in Canada. They
were both foreign students—she from Greece and he
from Ghana. He was working on his Ph.D. in civil engi-
neering, while our mother was completing her master's
in archeology. They fell in love, moved to the United
States and settled in Oregon. Dad traveled a lot. Then
one day he didn't come back. When he left, Lucian and
I took our mother's surname and nicknames. I was originally christened Basil. Mom preferred Basilio and so
do I."

"What about Lucian?"

"I think Dad used to call him Lucas. My mother
was always correcting him. 'It's Lucian, not Lucas.
He was named in honor of my grandfather,' she'd tell
him. I'm not sure how much he listened. Anyway, my
mother's family is enough for me. We have lots of rel-
atives on that side. All I remember was that our father
disappeared like a puff of smoke. Then one day our
mother told us he was dead. I was too young to remember much, but for Lucian...it hurt him. I remember my
father being a serious man who used to stay to himself.
I don't remember ever sitting on his lap, or him being
part of any of our family gatherings.

"But after he left, my mother remarried, and that's
the man who I considered to be my father. By then
Lucian was already out of the house, making money
and doing his best to forget him. There's no reminder
of our Ghanaian roots anywhere in his home. Lucian
doesn't want to remember Dad or Alana. So it's unusual
that you should have found that piece of material out of
nowhere."

"So you don't think your father's disappearance was
suspicious?"

"No. Fathers leave."

"I think there might be a connection," Callia said.

"And you have a wild imagination," Basilio said. "You think that all Ghanaians know each other?"

"No, I just—"

"What's done is done. What happened was unfortunate, but my brother is safe now. It was just a crazy woman out for revenge, nothing more. Whoever helped her probably thought she wanted to reconcile with my brother or something. I'm sure it was a harmless mistake. Alana could be very persuasive."

"Where were you when this happened?" Nikki asked.

Basilio hesitated. "I was away. Lucian sent me to the mainland to take care of some work."

"No," Callia said with a fierce shake of her head. "Uncle Lucian sent us away because he knew she would come."

"You don't know that," Basilio said in a harsh tone.

"Yes, I do. No one was in the house. No one else talked about escaping the fire. That means that everyone was sent away. Uncle was all alone."

"But you didn't know that then."

"I knew something wasn't right. I wanted to go back, but you didn't let me."

"But you went back, anyway," Basilio said. "And Lucian still blames me for that."

"I swear I don't know how it happened. I went to sleep and then woke up in the house."

"He suspects someone drugged us and took Callia back."

"Us?" said Nikki.

"Yes, I have a shaky memory of that night." Basilio turned away to look at the sea, clearly uncomfortable with the topic. "There's no use looking back. Alana was the cause of the fire and she's gone for good. Now there's nothing to worry about."

Nikki wanted to believe him, but the look on Callia's face made her question his blasé attitude. She sensed there was more to the story than he was telling her. But she didn't want to spoil the day.

"I'm sure you're right," she said.

"I know I am," Basilio said with a broad smile. "Let's go below deck and get some lunch."

Lunch was a welcomed diversion that consisted of a Greek salad; *imam bayildi*, or stuffed eggplant; and tomato pilaf—the fresh tomatoes lending a lovely pink hue to the rice—which were accompanied by more greens, yogurt cucumber sauce and smoked fish in almond sauce. One look at the appetizing feast wiped away Nikki's nagging thoughts. After the filling meal, Nikki returned to the sundeck and closed her eyes. But when she did, she saw Lucian's face, and behind him a fire roared.

Chapter 9

She was his dream and his torment, Lucian thought as he stood at his bedroom window and gazed down at Nikki, who stood on her balcony, looking sublimely serene and beautiful. For an instant he imagined showering her with rose petals, being beside her and gathering her close, pressing his mouth to hers, but he let those thoughts quickly fade away, knowing he could never be close to her. He saw her lift her head and take a deep breath and imagined her inhaling the scent of the sea and the fragrance of the flowers around her. Lucian briefly closed his eyes and imagined saying her name in the manner he wished to—as her lover. *Nikki. My darling Nikki.*

He opened his eyes and saw her turn her head, but he knew it was from the sound of the breeze whispering through the leaves, not because of him. She'd never answer to his call. He glanced down at his scarred hand, seeing its deformed ugliness. How could he have thought to reveal himself to her?

She created beauty. Was beauty. All she could offer him were apologies and pity. He couldn't—wouldn't— let himself get close again. Seared in his memory were the sound of her aborted scream and how she'd recoiled from his touch. At that moment he'd wanted to feel her soft skin against his even more. To have her desire him as a woman desired a man. But he'd been foolish to dream—foolish to hope. He'd been without a woman too long, Lucian tried to convince himself, and she'd just triggered a weakness. That was all. She was just a brief infatuation. She had to be.

Keeping her away not only kept him safe, but it kept her safe, too. He knew there was more to the night of the fire, and he was getting close to exacting his revenge. But there were still more things to do, and one more puzzle piece to uncover. No, he could pay to have a woman pretend to find him handsome and alluring, pay to keep her face from curling in disgust. He knew money could purchase a lot of things, and he also knew what his money couldn't buy. Lucian pressed his hand against the window and gazed at Nikki one more time before he turned away.

Basilio lay in bed and stared up into the darkness. Usually after a night of lovemaking he had no trouble falling asleep. Not tonight. How had a Ghanaian head wrap shown up for Nikki to find? And why did she mention Alana? He sensed an interest in her that seemed more than idle curiosity. He hated thinking of that night and having to lie, and Nikki had him asking himself questions he didn't want to ask. He hated questions with no quick answers. It was probably nothing.

He felt soft feminine arms circle him as Iona pressed her body against his.

"You're frowning again," she said.

"The lights are off. How can you tell?"

She traced his lips with her finger. "I just can. You're worried about something. What is it?"

Basilio shook his head. "Just work."

"So your brother still doesn't know about us?"

"If he did, I wouldn't be here," he said, referring to the empty villa where they met for their affair.

"You mean you'd leave me?"

"I mean you'd be out of a job and probably forced to find work on the mainland."

"Then I'm glad he doesn't know."

"I'll tell him soon."

"Not too soon," she said quickly. "I like what we have. It makes me feel safe. With no one knowing about us, no one can interfere."

"You have a point, but I hate keeping secrets from my brother."

Iona's hand slid down his thigh. "Even ones that feel this good?"

Basilio felt himself grow hard and his concerns and worries slipping away. "You have a point. I'm getting used to the idea."

She stroked him in his most tender place. "Tell me what's really bothering you."

He groaned. "How can I be bothered about anything when you're doing that?"

"Tell me," she whispered, her fingers stroking him even more and heightening his arousal.

"I was just thinking about the fire."

"Why? We all know what happened."

"Not everything." He reached for her. "No more questions."

She drew away slightly, confused. "Why are you thinking about the fire again?"

"Nikki asked me some questions about Alana."

"What kind of questions?"

"It doesn't matter now. You're driving me insane."

"She's an attractive woman."

Basilio didn't care. "I don't think about her like that. Only you. Always you."

"But—"

He stopped her with a kiss. He wanted Iona and could no longer take her teasing him. He drew her close and found sweet release between her legs. When it was over the second time, he was able to sleep. But he didn't dream about Iona.

Nikki returned to the house from a brisk morning jog and saw Iona in the hallway. She decided to be polite, so she smiled at her. "Good morning," she said in a bright voice.

"Morning," Iona replied coolly.

"I'm parched. Could you get me—"

"I don't take orders from you."

"Excuse me?" Nikki said, surprised by the woman's vehement refusal to fulfill such a simple request. "I thought you worked here."

"I don't work for you." She set down her duster and sauntered over to Nikki like a panther. "I see how you eye this house. You want to become mistress of it. You wouldn't be the first who wanted that."

Nikki stood firm, determined not to be intimidated, although there was something about the other woman that put her on edge. "I'm not here because of any romantic designs. I'm here because I was hired to do a job."

"Doesn't matter why you're here. You'll never be mistress. No woman will be. Mr. Kontos will never get over Alana."

"I think he can recover from a crazy woman who burns down his house."

Iona's lips thinned. "She wasn't crazy. She was murdered."

Nikki folded her arms to keep from trembling. *Murdered?* "By who?"

"Who else?"

"He wouldn't."

"He did."

"If you believe that, then why do you still work here?"

"I have nothing to fear. But you do. Don't stay here. It's a warning. Your only warning."

It didn't seem possible. Basilio had told her that people had their own version of events, but he'd never mentioned this one. But it was groundless. Nikki tossed the idea aside. Iona was just trying to frighten her because she didn't like her for some reason. She wouldn't let that intimidate her.

"You're not here to give warnings," Nikki said boldly, meeting Iona's stare. "You're here to work, and I'm sure getting me a drink is part of it."

Iona's eyes turned to onyx and her voice to ice. "You don't want to tangle with me. I told you. I don't take orders from you—"

"Since when?" a male voice cut in.

The two women turned and saw Dante coming around the corner. Nikki hadn't had much interaction with him. He was a solid, quiet figure who traveled through the house with intense purpose. Yet he didn't make her feel uneasy. He was always accommodating and kind. He had the kind of face that belonged on a bronze coin—imposing, regal, striking. He was of medium height but carried himself as if he were a foot taller. She'd learned that he was Italian, but he had none of their reputed charm. There was a rigid hardness about him that made him seem much older than a man in his late twenties.

His dark eyes met Iona's. His voice was firm. "You'll do as she asks."

"But I'm needed in the upper rooms," Iona said with an ingratiating smile. "Pardon me," she said, then gave a faux curtsy before slipping away.

Dante said something under his breath. Nikki couldn't make out the words but could imagine their meaning.

Nikki rubbed her arms, as if she'd just felt a cold blast. "She's awful. Why does Lucian keep her? Do you know that she thinks *he* killed Alana?"

"Silly rumors. I'm sorry about that and I apologize for her disrespect," Dante said in a curt, but polite tone, expertly sidestepping her questions. "What do you need?"

"I just wanted to get something to drink," Nikki said, remembering that she was thirsty. Something about Dante made her feel relaxed and at ease. "I just came back from a jog along the beach. It's so beautiful early in the morning. Don't worry," she said, wanting to stop a potential lecture. "I was careful, as Basilio warned."

"Warned?"

"Yes, he told me about the smugglers."

Dante gripped his hand into a fist, then relaxed it. "He shouldn't have told you about that. You don't have to worry about smuggling or any other criminal activity on this island. Kontos makes sure that all his guests are safe."

"I'm sure Basilio was just trying to be entertaining."

"Then he needs to try harder."

Nikki moved to the side, ready to leave. "I'll just go to my room and—"

Dante did the same, blocking her. "Are you sure you want only a drink?"

Nikki looked at him, curious.

"Because I could have a bath drawn for you," he hastily continued. "And perhaps I could have a morning snack prepared for you afterward, which I could have delivered to your room and have waiting on the balcony."

The man certainly knew how to please. "That would be wonderful."

He clasped his hands behind him and nodded. "If you have any more trouble with the staff or anyone, you let me know."

"I will," Nikki said, then went upstairs.

Dante watched her go, then walked outside and lit a cigarette. He then stopped and saw Basilio talking to a member of the staff of one of the other villas. He waited until the conversation was over before he approached him.

"What the hell is wrong with you?"

Basilio smiled. "Good morning to you, too."

Dante gritted his teeth. "You had no right frightening Nikki."

"You mean Ms. Rozan," Basilio said, reminding Dante of his position.

Dante took a long drag of his cigarette. "She allows me to call her by her given name."

"Lucky you," Basilio said in a mocking tone.

"Why is everything a joke to you?"

"It's not and I didn't frighten Nikki."

"You told her about smuggling."

Basilio paused. "It was nothing and I have better things to do than talk to you about it." He turned, bored with the conversation.

Dante grabbed his arm, his voice cold. "It was careless."

Basilio yanked his arm away. "Remember your place, Dante."

"I'll never forget it. I don't take anything for granted."

Basilio grinned. "And you think that I do?"

Dante stomped out his cigarette, wishing it was Basilio's face. He hated the man's smile. "I know that you do. And that will be your downfall."

Nikki strolled through the foyer after a relaxing shower and a delightful snack, feeling ready to start the day. She was making progress with her sketches, although the owner of the house was proving harder to pin down. It had been three days since the night on the terrace, and she hadn't seen him. She was thinking of this when she saw Callia, looking miserable as she sat in one of the empty rooms, stroking Pauline. Kay sat beside her, knitting.

Nikki walked over to the girl. "What's wrong?"

"My mother's coming."

Nikki hesitated. "And that's not a good thing?"

"No."

"When is she coming?"

"In a month. I don't want to see her, but if I have to, please don't leave me alone with her."

"I'm sure it will be fine. You'll have Kay. I may not be here." Nikki knew her days would end sooner than expected if something didn't change. Lucian had ignored her request to speak to him about her designs. He was making her job as difficult as possible.

"You'll be here," Callia said without concern. "Please stay when she comes. You can pretend to be measuring a wall or something. Just don't leave me with her."

"All right," Nikki agreed, although she didn't think there was anything she could do. "But if she asks me to leave, I'll have to."

"She won't even notice you." Callia pulled out her cell phone and sent a message. "She never notices staff."

Dante appeared, apparently responding to Callia's message. "Yes?" he said.

Callia put her phone away. "When my mother comes, where will you put her when she first arrives?"

"The sitting room off to the—"

Callia shook her head. "No, make it the conservatory, please."

"Okay." Dante nodded.

"And no drinks until the late afternoon."

"But if she asks—"

"Tell her you're out and need to get a new supply. She'll believe you."

Dante raised his brows, amused. "Any more instructions?"

"No. Nikki will be with me, pretending to work. After an hour give us an excuse to leave."

"Now, Ms. Callia—"

"Dante, please."

"You should respect your mother more," Kay said.

Callia turned to her. "No one asked you."

"Manners, Callia," Kay said softly, unfazed by the girl's rudeness.

Callia gripped her hands. "Why does she have to come here? It's bad enough that I have to travel to see her four times a year. But why is Uncle Lucian letting her come here and spoil things?"

"She insisted," Dante said.

"The cow," Callia grumbled.

Kay wagged a finger. "That's not nice."

"She's not coming tomorrow," Dante said. "So stop being unhappy about it. Let Kay take you to Italy for a week."

"Can you come?"

"No. I have work to do," Dante replied.

Callia frowned. "You're always working."

"That's because I have a lot to do."

"You didn't before. You, Uncle and I used to travel to Italy and Spain just for fun. Sometimes you'd just take me to the mainland and we'd have ices and—"

"Basilio can take you."

"He's not the same. You work too hard and that's why you don't smile."

Dante tweaked her chin. "I'd rather see you smile. Chef is making one of your favorite desserts."

She sat up with interest. "Which one?"

"Why don't you come and see?"

Kay spoke up. "I don't think that's appropriate. She's not a little girl anymore."

"I don't see the harm in it," Nikki said, seeing the disappointment on Callia's face.

"You wouldn't understand," Kay replied.

"She's right," Dante said. Then his phone rang

before anyone could argue. "Pardon me," he said, then walked out.

Callia watched him leave and Nikki could see the longing in the young woman's eyes. Yes, Callia was at the right age to develop a crush, and Dante was completely blind to her affection. Perhaps Kay was right to keep Callia "above" stairs, because nothing could come from the young woman's infatuation. Nikki waited, expecting Callia to say something rude or get angry at Kay. Instead she sat quietly, with tears streaming down her face.

Nikki stretched out her hand to her. "Let's go for a walk. It's okay, Kay. I'll take care of her."

The two wandered outside and walked a distance in silence. Then Callia said in a quiet voice, "Dante doesn't like me anymore."

"I'm sure that's not true."

"We used to be such good friends. It was Uncle Lucian, Dante and me. Then Basilio came, and now Kay, and he avoids me because he thinks I'm crazy."

"He has a lot of responsibilities and you're not a little girl anymore."

"I know. I'll be fifteen next month. If I were older, I'd make Dante want me."

Nikki paused, surprised by Callia's brazen statement. "But you're not." She wanted to be gentle with the young woman's feelings but knew that the situation couldn't be what she wanted it to be. "I remember my first crush. A teacher. I thought my heart would break when he got married, but I got over it, and you will, too. You have a lot of growing up to do, and things change in relationships."

Callia wiped her eyes and sniffed. "I'll always love Dante."

"Yes, maybe your love will change into something else."

"Uncle Lucian hates me to talk about the past, but sometimes I like it better there. Uncle says, 'It's not where you've been it's where you're going.'"

"That's right."

"Then why do I sometimes feel that everything that's important to me is going away?"

Chapter 10

Nikki crumpled up a wad of paper and tossed it aside in frustration. Dante had kindly set her up in the room she was to design, providing a small drafting table and all the supplies she needed. It didn't help. Her ideas weren't coming together. She'd never had this much trouble with a design before. And she had no one to blame but herself. Callia had given her great ideas, as had Basilio. The last several evenings he'd been extra courteous, making her stay pleasant. He made up for Lucian's absence.

"He usually eats alone," Basilio said several nights ago at dinner.

Callia opened her mouth to say something, then winced and closed it.

Nikki suspected he was lying, and understood. Since the night on the terrace she'd seen Lucian only in passing and was never given a chance to be alone with him.

While one brother avoided her, the other went out of his way to charm her. Even last night at dinner she'd tried to ignore Lucian's absence and enjoy the *garides me feta*—sautéed shrimp dressed in a ruby-red tomato sauce, sprinkled with feta cheese and served with loads of crusty bread with which to soak up the succulent juices. For dessert they had had Turkish dried apricots stuffed with cream that were lightly covered with syrup and sprinkled with pistachios.

After dinner Basilio had strolled with Nikki in the garden. "I didn't mean to upset you about the smugglers," he'd said. "Dante told me I did and I apologize."

"No need. When I mentioned it to him, I didn't think he would take it so seriously."

Basilio scowled. "Dante takes everything seriously."

"You've really made my time here enjoyable."

"I'm glad."

As she sat at her drafting table, Nikki could not avoid the fact that despite Basilio's efforts, Lucian still loomed large, as did the mysterious Alana. How could she please a man who kept her locked out? Not that she blamed him, after the awful encounter on the terrace. She knew this design meant more than she wanted it to. It was an apology and a plea for him to trust her once more. She took out a new sheet of paper and started again.

The cat, Lethe, came into the room and jumped up on the table.

"Shoo," Nikki said with a wave of her hand.

He blinked.

Nikki sighed. "All these other flat surfaces and you have to choose here?" She nudged him. He growled. She snatched her hand away. "I thought you were supposed to be friendly."

He licked his paw, then looked at her again.

Nikki held up her hands in surrender. "Okay, you win. You can stay."

He curled into a ball, looking as soft and cuddly as a tiger.

She rested her chin in her hand and studied him, wishing he could talk. "What can you tell me about your owner?"

"He thinks people who talk to animals are strange," a voice said behind her.

She spun in her chair, stunned, not knowing what to say. Lucian seemed casual and relaxed, as if nothing had happened between them and those days of avoidance were a trifle. That made her even more uneasy, because she knew he was a man who didn't forget anything.

"I never asked you about your trip with Basilio."

"You haven't been around to ask."

"I'm asking now. Did you two enjoy yourselves?"

"Callia was there, too," she said, annoyed by his insinuation.

"And you had a good time?"

"A very good time." She cleared her throat, but her voice remained hoarse. "What do you want?"

"I want to see how things are progressing." He glanced at the paper balls on the floor. "It looks like they're not."

"I have my own system," Nikki said, trying to show a nonchalance she didn't feel.

Lucian picked up a paper ball. "It seems broken."

"I've requested to see you and get your feedback, but you've been oddly out of reach."

"Feel like quitting?"

"I wouldn't give you the pleasure."

Lucian began to open the paper ball.

Nikki grabbed his hands. "That's not for you to see."

He stiffened and his eyes met hers in a silent challenge. Their gazes held each other in a battle of wills. She felt the strength of his hands, hers almost looking like a child's in comparison. She knew she could fight him, but she wouldn't win. He wouldn't be the first to let go. Nikki sighed and she reluctantly did. He opened the crumpled paper and spread it out on the table. He studied it for a moment, his expression giving nothing away. Then he bent down and took another scrunched-up paper off the floor and did the same, then another.

Nikki watched him with growing impatience, then stomped her foot. "At least say something. Do you hate them? Like them? Don't care?" She rested her hand on the stack of paper. "Give me something."

Lucian removed her hand, rested his arms on the table and continued to ignore her.

"I'm sorry, okay? That night on the terrace wasn't what you thought and—"

He held up a hand, while keeping his gaze focused on her sketches. "I'm not here for that." He sent her a sharp look. "Don't bring it up again."

Nikki sighed, knowing that was impossible. What had happened hung between them. At least on her end. She couldn't compartmentalize the way he could. She wanted to touch his scarred hand and caress the raised skin on his neck. She wanted to massage the tension in his shoulders. She had found something else to do with her fingers when she suddenly felt a strange vibration. She glanced down and saw she'd been stroking Lethe, who'd begun to purr loudly. She yanked her hand back.

As the silence stretched between them, her sympathy for Lucian was replaced with frustration. Was this how he meant to punish her? It didn't take this long to form an opinion about her work. Was he taking the time to come up with a suitable cutting remark? Fine. She'd be prepared for it.

She began to pace. "You're exasperating," she muttered to herself, not caring if he heard her or not. "No wonder the others quit. This was supposed to be my dream assignment. I can't tell you how much I dreamed of seeing inside this house. But of course, there's not much to see. Instead there are shadows behind every door, rude maids, mysterious butlers, flirtatious brothers, a strange girl and an owner who barely speaks to me for nearly a week, then shows up, expecting a masterpiece."

"Are you finished?"

Nikki halted, turned to Lucian and found him watching her, amused.

She folded her arms, embarrassed, but gave a careless toss of her head. "Yes."

Lucian sat back. "No meze table is absolutely complete without *dolmades*—stuffed grape leaves. It is my favorite…" He waved his hand, searching for a word. "What's the word? Starter? Breaker?"

"Appetizer?"

"Yes, appetizer. I love the fresh tomatoes and aubergines."

"Aubergines?"

"Yes, the purple vegetable."

"Eggplant?"

He nodded. "And courgettes, what you call zucchini. The grape leaves are stuffed with rice and these vegetables and served with lemon wedges and yogurt. Have you ever had them?"

Nikki shook her head, not sure where he was going with his story.

"I'll make sure you have some before you leave. Anyway, I once had a chef who knew that I loved this dish and added extra cinnamon, olive oil and yellow onions. He also cooked the leaves until they wilted. It was too much and I didn't enjoy it. Can you guess why?"

"I'm sure you'll tell me."

"Because he was trying too hard to impress me. He forgot to do his job, which was to prepare *dolmades* and nothing more. I don't need to be impressed." He stood. "It will make things easier."

"How can things be easy when you go out of your way to avoid me? You don't join us for dinner. I have asked Dante for an appointment with you and have been told you're too busy."

"Because I am."

"But the other night can't be—"

Lucian's eyes and tone hardened. "The other night meant nothing, was nothing, is nothing."

Nikki blinked as if he'd slapped her. "Then why can't *I* forget it? Why won't you forgive me?"

"How can I forgive you when there's nothing to forgive?"

Nikki threw up her hands. "I hate these word games you play."

"Good. We now understand each other." He patted Lethe. "He likes you."

"But you don't."

Lucian only gave her an enigmatic look before walking away.

Nikki gripped her hands into fists and shook them in the air, then sank into her chair, feeling as if an anvil had just fallen on her. He'd effectively demolished the beauty of the time they'd shared on the terrace by not letting her speak of it. Nothing happened. What he was really saying was that she didn't matter. That she was one of a number of women who'd come and gone from his life. Why did she care? There were plenty of other men.

She'd returned Benjamin's ring with a note, unable to pretend that their relationship was more than it was. She knew he'd be relieved. His actions had been impulsive. He was more afraid of losing her than he was desirous of building a new future with her. She wanted to think that she could just return to the carefree relationship she'd had with him, but she knew that would be impossible. Lucian stood in her way. She didn't want to think about him, but she couldn't help herself. But if he didn't care, neither would she.

Nikki briefly covered her eyes, feeling defeated. Not only had Lucian rejected her as a lover, but he also hadn't liked her designs. She needed to focus on her job, complete it, then leave. Nikki opened her eyes and stared down at her sketches. He was right. They were too ostentatious and showy. She was embarrassed that her desperation had shown. She had wanted to impress him with her brilliance, but she'd failed.

She seemed to be failing a lot lately. Nikki abruptly stood, startling Lethe. "I don't care if he thinks I'm strange talking to you. You're the only one who seems to make sense around here. Can you make me forget?" She reached out and stroked him, no longer afraid. He brushed his head against her hand. She scratched him behind the ears and he began to purr. "At least I can make you happy." She glanced around the room, feeling as if the walls were closing in on her. "I need to get out of here."

And as if he understood her, Lethe jumped down and walked to the door.

"You want to come with me? Fine. I'll accept the company."

Chapter 11

She usually kept her walks to the day but liked the quiet of the dying light as evening came, and Lethe made a nice companion. Nikki stopped on the beach and sat down on a rock, listening to the soft sounds of the waves creeping up the shore. She petted Lethe, who suddenly became watchful.

"How much longer must I wait?" a familiar voice asked from somewhere in the trees.

Nikki turned and saw Iona with her arm around Basilio's neck. Nikki glanced around for a hiding place, then darted behind a boulder so that she wouldn't be spotted by them.

"Be patient," Basilio said.

"I thought you loved me."

"I do," he said, then lowered his head to kiss her.

Nikki winced at the sight. *Basilio and Iona? What an awful combination on so many levels.* Yes, physically they made an attractive couple, but their temperaments were so different. Basilio could have any woman he wanted. Why would he choose his brother's impertinent maid? But this new knowledge helped explain Iona's saucy attitude. Did she expect to marry into the family one day and be the one giving orders? Nikki shivered at the thought and moved closer to the boulder. She stepped on a piece of driftwood.

Basilio looked around. "What was that?"

"Nothing," Iona said.

"Quiet. I heard something."

"Silly boy. You'd jump at the wind. Now, will you—"

"No."

"Not even for me?"

"Things are going well and I don't want to change that."

"It's that woman," Iona spat out. "She's changed your mind about me."

"That's not true."

"You spend your evenings with her and take her out."

"I have to."

"No, you don't. You do it because you like her company."

"That's true, but I want no one else but you."

"Then do as I ask," she said, then kissed him and ran away.

Basilio sighed, then soon followed.

Nikki waited a few moments, then crept out of her hiding place. She glanced down at Lethe and shook her head. "That sight completely ruined my evening." She glanced at the horizon, having missed most of the beauty of the sunset, and headed up the beach.

Strong arms seized her and a hand clamped over her

mouth. "Promise not to scream?" Basilio said in a dark voice.

She nodded.

He removed his left hand and spun her around, keeping his right hand on her arm. Fierce eyes bored into hers, the smiling, charming Basilio replaced with a man who scared her. "What are you doing out here this late?" he demanded.

Nikki swallowed. "I was just walking."

"Not spying?"

"Why would I spy?"

He hesitated, as if processing her reply, "What did you see?"

"Nothing."

He shook her. "Don't lie to me. Tell me what you saw."

"I just saw you with Iona."

He glanced behind him. "And how much did you hear?"

"Nothing I could really understand," Nikki said, getting angry. "What's going on? What are you doing with her?"

"Stop asking questions. Just do what you came to do."

"She thinks your brother is a murderer. Did you know that?"

"There are some things you don't understand."

"She sounded pretty clear to me."

"It's nothing. Stop trying to find a mystery that isn't there." He lowered his voice. "Don't tell anyone what you saw or heard tonight. Understand?"

"Yes."

His grip tightened painfully but Nikki didn't cry out. "Especially Lucian. Do you hear me?"

Nikki nodded, truly seeing how strong his feelings for Iona were. "Okay."

"Promise."

"I promise."

He released her and walked away. Nikki shivered. She'd seen his dark side, a part of him that terrified her. What had he been doing out this late? What did Iona want him to do? Why would Basilio be with her? Did he believe her? Why did her questions upset him? She sensed that danger was lurking, but had no idea about the nature of it. She wouldn't say anything until she found out more.

From several yards away a ghost of white smoke danced up to the moon. Dante stared at the head of his cigarette, then shifted his gaze back to Nikki as she quickly made her way back to the mansion. Then he looked at Basilio, who was headed in the opposite direction. He'd watch him even more now. He knew he couldn't be trusted. Dante calmly inhaled his cigarette as he thought of his next move. He knew he should tell Lucian, but now wasn't the time. There was still too much at stake. He would be patient and wait for Basilio to give him what he wanted.

Nikki returned to the mansion and thought of running into her room and hiding there, but her sketches called her instead. Work. She needed to work and then she wouldn't feel so frightened. She walked down the hall, then stopped when she saw Lucian standing in the doorway of the room where her sketches were, with his back to her. It was too soon. Her emotions were too close to the surface for her to see him again. She took a hasty step back.

But he turned and saw her. Their eyes met, and for one raw, unguarded moment she saw the hurt, fear and pain in his dark green eyes and it broke her heart. Then, in an instant, it was gone. But it was too late. The sight had seared itself into her mind, and she could no longer see him as a cold, distant tycoon, but as a man who needed to heal, and she desperately wanted to be the woman to help him.

He frowned, his eyes searching hers. "Is something wrong?"

Yes. "No." She took another step back, ready to run.

His frown deepened. "Did you need something?" he asked in a sharp, probing tone.

"No." She flung her hand out in a helpless gesture. She was just recovering from his brother's anger. She couldn't handle his, too. "I just wanted to look at the room again, but…"

"I can leave, if you want to be alone."

"No," she said quickly, almost desperately. "I'll come back later. I'm sorry I disturbed you."

Lucian crossed the hallway in long strides, moving faster than she'd expected. "You didn't disturb me." He seized her arm but snatched his hand back when she cried out. "You're hurt." He lifted her arm and looked at the bruise. "What happened?"

Nikki glanced down, surprised to see the mark. "Nothing."

"You're a bad liar. Now come with me," he replied, ushering her into the room.

Nikki absently rubbed the bruise on her arm and followed him. "I just went on a walk, and it got dark and I fell."

"That lie is even worse than the first." His thumb brushed across the bruise. "Who did this?"

"I just told you—"

Lucian held up his hand. "No more lies, Nikki. Tell me what really happened."

"I startled someone, and he pushed me aside and ran off."

Lucian took a deep breath, controlling his temper. "Who?"

"It was dark." She searched her mind for a good story. "Basilio told me there are smugglers—"

Lucian gritted his teeth. "Not on my island. Not anymore. Who did you see?"

"Maybe another guest staying in one of the villas. It was dark. Please," she begged. "It was nothing."

He raised his hand to her face, then let it fall before touching her cheek. "*Nothing* has you near tears?"

Nikki blinked the tears away, but several fell, anyway. She brushed them aside. "I just had an unhappy thought."

"Did someone threaten you?"

"No."

"And yet you're frightened."

"Yes, I'm frightened that I'll fail and that you'll send me away without giving me a chance to finish."

"Hmm. That lie sounds more convincing."

"It's true."

"You should never have come here," he said, half to himself. "I should send you back—"

"No, please don't," Nikki said, understanding why Callia didn't want to leave him. Until she learned more, she wasn't sure he was safe. "Let me finish what I came to do. You're right. I was trying to impress you, but I'll do better now."

His steady gaze remained on her face. "You're trying to distract me." He bit his lip. "Since I can't get you to tell me the truth, perhaps I can get Basilio to persuade you. He's more—"

Nikki shook her head. "No, I told you it was nothing." She saw the doubt in his eyes and turned away, desperate to change the subject. "Tell me what happened in this room."

Her statement had its desired effect. Lucian paused, and the doubt and worry in his eyes turned into something else. He turned and pointed. "Right over there I asked Alana to marry me." Lucian sent Nikki a significant look. "By now you've heard about her."

Nikki nodded. "And what did she say?"

"What else would a woman say to a man as rich as I am? She said yes, with gold shining in her eyes and silver running through her veins." He gripped his cane. "Soon after, I found her in bed with one of my patrolmen and broke off the engagement. She begged me to forgive her. She told me that she really loved me. I didn't bend, because there had been rumors of other men. She pleaded with me, saying how much her father admired me. It hurt, because I admired him, too. He'd become like my own father." Lucian stopped and sighed. "That's when things changed," he said, remembering that day.

He'd left her room and headed downstairs. Alana had grabbed a robe and followed him. She grabbed his arm to stop him.

"You don't know what you're saying."

He yanked himself free of her grasp. "Of course I do."

"I understand that you're upset."

Lucian turned around and laughed. "Upset?"

"But you don't know all that's at risk. Let's talk about this."

"It's over." He walked into the dining room and sat down for lunch. A maid set a plate in front of him. "The staff knew I was returning early. Unfortunately, no one warned you."

"It was just a moment of weakness. You've been away and I was so lonely. He seduced me."

"In your own bedroom?"

"You can't just get rid of me. No one gets rid of me. I know too much. I can hurt the people you love."

Lucian picked up his knife. "And live to regret it."

She rushed toward him. "You can't throw away all that we've meant to each other. All that we've built together." She touched him, and he felt himself respond, but then remembered the same fingers caressing the face of the patrolman. He moved away. "No. I want you and your family gone by tonight."

"Please don't shame me like this. Not this way."

"Then you can break up with me and save face."

"My father would never understand."

"Make him understand. Lie. You're good at that."

She slapped him.

He cupped her chin. "You're lucky you're a woman. I'll let that pass. Now, get out of my house."

"You'll pay. I'll make you suffer."

Lucian shook his head at the memory, her words clearly echoing in his mind. "And she got back at me for breaking off the engagement," he told Nikki. He lowered his head and sighed. "I suffered in ways I didn't think possible. I'd allowed her the luxury of her own bank account and helped her develop two foundations. I discovered that she had not only betrayed me with another man, but had also embezzled from the foundations and given money to her father to help rebels in southern Belgona try to overtake the government. My name was suddenly tied to guerrilla warfare, massacres and greed. I scrambled to save what entities I could, but many of my African subsidiaries distanced themselves from me, and even some of my European ones. I have struggled since to rebuild those alliances.

"But that wasn't all she wanted. She wanted to destroy even more. And I learned—" He abruptly stopped and shook his head. "No, I don't want to remember any more."

"Did you know she would start the fire?" Nikki asked gently. "Is that why you sent Callia with Basilio to the mainland?"

"I knew something would happen."

Did you murder her? Nikki thought, then quickly brushed the thought aside. He wasn't that kind of man. "She could have killed you."

"By that time I didn't care anymore, and if Callia hadn't been in the house…" He let his words trail off.

"She doesn't remember how she got there."

"I know. She was obviously put there by someone."

"I'm glad she was."

Lucian stared at her, confused. "But she could have gotten killed."

"Instead she ended up saving your life."

Lucian glanced down at the scars on his hand. "I still wonder if it was worth saving."

Nikki raised his hand to her lips and kissed the scars. "I think it was," she whispered, then kissed the ones on his neck and brushed her lips against his. "Let me kiss all your scars and the ones that don't exist."

"That's a tempting offer."

"That offer doesn't last forever."

"How long does it last?"

"Lucian," Basilio called, breaking the mood. Nikki

moved away from Lucian as his brother entered. He glanced at them, unsure. "Am I interrupting something?"

"No," Lucian said in a brusque voice. He walked past Basilio and said over his shoulder, "What is it?"

Basilio glanced at Nikki and she saw the silent question in his eyes: Did she tell Lucian anything?

She shook her head, and he nodded, then followed his brother.

Once they were gone, Nikki looked around the stark room, and everything came into focus. She clearly saw what the room needed. How it should feel, what it should look like. Not just this room, but the others as well. She knew what Lucian needed, what Callia needed. They needed a *home*. Presently the mansion was dead, haunted by painful memories, but she would help it come alive again. Return it to a time when they were both happy. She also knew how she would shatter the walls Lucian had built around his heart and teach him to trust love again. Her love would save him.

Love? Nikki paused at the word. Did she love him? *Yes.* She didn't expect to, but somehow she did. It seemed right. The thought didn't scare her; instead it settled in her heart. Yes, her mind told her, it was impulsive and reckless, but her heart didn't care. The redesigned room would be her love letter to Lucian.

Chapter 12

Renewed, Nikki decided to go to her room and relax. She halted when she saw Iona standing by her bed.

"What are you doing?"

"Changing your sheets."

"I didn't ask for them to be changed."

"I changed them, anyway," Iona said, lifting the old sheets from off the floor.

Determined not to be intimidated, Nikki walked past her and sat in front of her vanity. She removed her earrings.

"You can't compete, you know," Iona said.

Nikki paused. "Compete?"

"Alana was more than you could ever be. She filled every corner of his heart. She will not be easily erased."

"You need to get your story straight. If he loved her so much, why did he kill her?"

Iona laughed. "Wouldn't you like to know?"

"I bet you don't."

"He couldn't have her, that's why."

"Lucian doesn't strike me as a jealous man."

"Then you know nothing."

Nikki met Iona's cool gaze in the mirror. "Goodbye."

Iona shrugged. "Just trying to save you from heart-break."

"It's not *my* heartbreak you should worry about."

Iona's arrogant stance wavered. "What do you mean?"

Nikki turned. "Who will Basilio ultimately choose? You or his brother?"

Iona's face turned red.

"I won't say a word, as long as you behave." Nikki pointed to a tossed pillowcase on the floor. "Don't forget that."

Iona sent her one last glare, snatched up the pillow-case, then stormed out.

Nikki stared at her bed, no longer feeling comfortable in her room. She didn't trust Iona and didn't like her presence. She knew she wouldn't be able to sleep, so she returned to her drafting table downstairs and started to work on her new ideas. She worked all through the night and into the morning. Nikki woke when she heard the clatter of dishes. She opened her eyes and saw Dante setting down a tray. She sat up and stretched. His handsome face was a pleasant sight to see in the morning, and she could understand why poor Callia had a crush on him.

"I'm sorry," he said. "I didn't mean to wake you."

"That's okay." She glanced at her watch. "It's about time, anyway." She looked at the tray. "Hmm, that smells delicious."

He glanced at the table. "Is everything coming along?"

Nikki grinned and covered her sketches, suddenly getting an idea. "Yes. Wait right here. Don't peek."

When he nodded, she ran to her bedroom, freshened up and changed, then returned to Dante, who remained quietly sitting at her drafting table.

"Did you peek?"

He looked offended. "You told me not to."

She uncovered the images. "What do you think?"

He sent a look to her tray. "Your food's getting cold. Do you want me to get you another dish?"

"Don't worry about that," she said with impatience. "Just look and tell me what you think."

He hesitated. "It's not my place to give opinions."

"I'm asking you because I trust you. Please."

Dante sighed, then looked impressed. "It's amazing. You think you can do this?"

"With the right help. I was thinking that I would surprise Lucian, instead of showing him. Do you think I should?"

"Yes."

Nikki bit her lip. "You don't think he'll be angry?"

"I'll deal with that."

"We'll need carpenters and painters and—"

"I can provide you with whatever you need."

"It's short notice."

"That won't be a problem."

"Thanks." Nikki smiled and hugged him, then drew back. "I'm sorry. I know I'm not supposed to do that."

He flashed a quick grin. "I won't tell anyone."

"How come you're not married?" Nikki asked, surprised by how even a small smile lit up his face.

"How come you're not?"

"Too focused on my career."

"Me too."

"And you leave the women around the world weeping."

He laughed, then said, "I have an idea." He picked up a pencil. "May I?"

"Yes."

He altered a sketch, then waited.

"That's perfect," Nikki said, surprised by his skill.

"Callia likes windows."

Nikki thought of mentioning Callia's feelings for him but knew that would be unfair. In a few months she'd grow out of it. "She'll love this."

Instead of offering her another smile, Dante abruptly set the pencil down and straightened. "Basilio's coming."

"How do you know?"

"I can smell him," he said, then quickly corrected himself. "I mean, his footsteps are distinctive."

"Ah, that's where you are," Basilio said, strolling in with his hands in his pockets. "What are you two looking at?"

"My design for this room," Nikki said.

He walked toward her. "Great. Let me see."

She folded the papers over. "No, it's a surprise."

"But you showed him," he said, gesturing to Dante.

"Because he knows how to keep secrets."

"So do I."

"And she needs my help," Dante said.

"I can help. I'm the reason she's here in the first place."

"Congratulations," Dante said in a dry tone. He looked at Nikki. "I'll make some calls."

She didn't want to be left alone with Basilio yet. "Can it wait? I have a few more questions."

"Okay." Dante nodded.

She offered Basilio a smile of apology. "If you'll excuse us."

Basilio hesitated, then left.

Nikki sat behind her drafting table, trying to settle her nerves. She didn't hear Dante move until he shifted her papers aside and placed the tray in front of her.

"Thank you," she said absently.

"He makes you nervous."

"It's probably just nerves. I don't want to disappoint him, either."

"You won't. Eat and you'll feel better."

She took a spoonful of the sweet and colorful fruit salad.

"I know you saw him with Iona on the beach," Dante said.

Nikki looked at him. "You do?"

"Yes, I was there too."

"I didn't expect him to be so angry."

Dante nodded, looking grim. "Basilio likes to hide his temper behind a smile. He fools a lot of people."

"But not you."

"When you work for people, you get to know them."

"I know that Lucian depends on you for a lot more than house duties. He trusts you to maintain the villas and the safety of the island. Has the smuggling really stopped?"

"Yes. You are safe."

Nikki wondered if he was telling her the truth or just saying what he thought she wanted to hear.

"That's good to know. Basilio seemed to hint that there's still activity."

"Basilio likes to court trouble."

Like Iona? Could he have been the one to let Alana in? It was only recently that the two brothers had reconnected. How close were they, really? And what was he up to? He could have so many women. Why one of the maids? His brother's maid. A maid who thought Lucian had murdered his ex-fiancée.

"If Lucian were to die, who inherits?" she asked.

"Most of his money goes to Callia and then Basilio."

"So with Callia out of the way, all of it would go to Basilio."

"I know what you're thinking."

Nikki briefly closed her eyes. "It's awful, isn't it?"

"No, I've thought about it myself. Lucian would never think his brother would betray him. That leaves him vulnerable, but I look at all options."

"But if Basilio meant to hurt him, why would he bring me here?"

"I haven't figured that out yet."

"A man has a right to have a bad temper when he's trying to protect the woman he loves," Nikki said, trying to be fair. "I can't believe Basilio would—"

"Resort to murder?"

"Yes."

Dante nodded. "Me neither. But I watch him all the same." He rubbed his forehead. "Your presence here means a lot to all of us. Please believe that Lucian and I will do everything in our power to make sure you're safe."

"I know."

He gave a curt nod, then left.

Nikki let out a sigh, feeling better that she had someone to confide in. She was safe. Dante would make sure of it. And she was sure Basilio was harmless. He was just a young man in love. It was ridiculous to be afraid of him.

Nikki finished her sketches, then went out on the terrace. She saw Basilio there and hesitated, unsure she wanted to talk to him, then moved forward, deciding to give him another chance. "Hello," she said.

He stood and held out a chair. "I'm sorry about the other night. I didn't mean to frighten you."

"It's okay." She wanted to believe him, but his cordial manner seemed a bit practiced. Had Dante told him to apologize?

"Would you like to go out on the water again?"

"Not today. I really have a lot of work to do."

"Maybe another time?"

"Yes, maybe," she said, a little sad that the fun between them had died. He sensed it, too, and they sat together in silence.

"If you won't go for her, I will," Dante said, catching Lucian watching Nikki as she lazed on the terrace. They could see her from the study window.

"She's cast a spell on you, too?" Lucian said with a laugh.

"Don't sound surprised. I may be your butler, but I'm also a man."

Lucian turned to him. "You know you're a lot more than a butler."

"Think she'll have me?"

"You don't have any money."

"She doesn't care about money."

Lucian sighed and went to his desk. "I know."

"Or station. Most American women don't."

"And what do you know about American women?" Lucian said, amused.

Dante gave a sly grin. "Enough." He looked at Nikki. "Take the risk. She won't be here for long, and I know it's been a while for you."

"You're a bad influence. You're supposed to be warning me away."

"Warn you away from making love to a beautiful, sexy woman?" Dante tapped his chest. "What kind of friend would I be?"

"I'm not sure."

"So she can go ahead with the project?"

Lucian shrugged. "How can I refuse?"

Dante raised a sly eyebrow. "Exactly."

Kay paced as she listened to the voice on the line. "I don't think we should." She gripped the phone, knowing the owner of the voice was watching her, but not knowing from where. "Nikki knows now."

"There's nothing she can do."

"I saw her talking to Dante."

"Dante only thinks he knows something. You leave him to me. You can't back out now. You're in too deep."

"I can pay you the money back."

"It would take you years. We've come too far."

"You promise no one gets hurt?"

"That's right. Just continue to watch the girl and report anything to me."

Chapter 13

Almost overnight construction on the room began—carpenters, painters, sculptors were shipped in and started working. Nikki had also ordered furniture, which would be expedited and would arrive within days. She learned quickly that the mention of the Kontos name made things happen. But Nikki also knew that meant her time on the island would come to an end soon, and she needed to convince Lucian to let her stay.

You can't compete. Iona's words haunted her, as did the memory of Alana, but she wouldn't let either woman stop her. She might not win, but she would at least try. She would fight.

Nikki prepared herself for the battle as she walked down to a private spot on the beach where she knew Lucian liked to swim. It was evening and the pink rays of the sun, with its weakening light, touched the white sand, the blue water and the tops of trees. At first she saw nothing but an empty stretch of beach. Then she saw him: a silhouette in the distance, emerging out of the water.

She set her towel down, took off her robe and walked up to the water's edge, ready to get in and surprise him, but he was too alert for that. He turned to her and for a moment didn't move, as if he was trying to assess if she was real, and then he swam toward her.

She smiled. "I wasn't sure Callia was telling me the truth, but it seems she was. Mind if I join you?" She took a step forward, then noticed his robe and trunks next to his cane off to the side. Obviously Callia hadn't told her everything—such as her uncle's preference for swimming in the nude. Nikki had to play it cool.

Lucian noticed her glance. "It seems you're a bit overdressed." He stood, taking care to remain where the water met his waist, but with just a few more steps he could give her a different view.

"Maybe you're underdressed."

He rested his hands on his hips. "I set the rules. It's my island."

Nikki set her robe aside but didn't remove her bikini. She slowly descended into the water. "And what happens when someone breaks the rules?"

"They regret it."

"Really?" she said in a coy voice. "Are your punishments severe?"

He lifted one shoulder. "That depends."

She stopped a few feet away from him. "On what?"

"The rule breaker."

"I'm not worried."

Lucian folded his arms. "What are you doing here?"

"I'm here to turn you back into a man. You didn't let me last time."

"And you think now will be different?"

"Yes."

His emerald gaze held her still. His voice calm and steady, he said, "You still haven't told me your price, sorceress."

"I told you there is no price."

"And I don't believe you."

"You will."

Lucian held out his arms to the side. "You think this beast you see before you can become a man again?"

"I believe he already is one, but I have to convince him of it."

"Hmm. You'll have to catch me first." He took a step back, then disappeared under the water.

Nikki rushed forward but couldn't see anything. "Lucian, that's not fair." She waited, but he didn't re-emerge. "What are you? A fish?" she grumbled, surprised by how long he could hold his breath. She took a gulp of air, ready to go under the water and search for him, when he popped up behind her.

He grinned. "You're not even trying."

She spun around and lunged for him, but he easily slipped out of her grasp. He dove under the water and within seconds emerged several feet away from her. He moved at lightning speed. On land he was slow and awkward, but in the water he had the power of Poseidon. She felt and sensed that he reveled in his power in the sea. That was why he enjoyed the water. He was the man he'd once been. No limp, no weakness, no limits.

"I will catch you," she said, then dove into the water and swam in his direction, but when she came up for a breath, he was yards away in another direction.

"Take off your top," Lucian said, "and I'll make it easier for you."

Her heart thundered in her chest. "And if I say no?"

Her question was met by silence. Then he suddenly popped up behind her, his breath warm on her skin. "And why would you say no?" He tugged on the back of her bikini top. "I noticed you're no longer wearing Benjamin's ring."

"Yes."

"Does he know that?"

"Yes, I gave him my answer."

"What was it?"

"I told him that it would never work."

"Why?"

"Because there's someone else."

"Hmm." Lucian loosened the string of her top.

"Stop that," she said when he began to remove it. "I can undress myself."

"So what? I like doing this."

"Even if I don't want you to?"

"You want me to, or you wouldn't still be here." He tossed her top away.

"Wait!" Nikki reached out, frantically trying to grab it. "It will float out into the ocean." She lunged for it.

Lucian wrapped his arm around her waist and held her still. "What a wonderful souvenir for someone to find."

"And what about me?" she said, covering her chest. "Now I have nothing. Why did you do that?"

His voice dropped to a husky whisper. "I'm a beast, remember?"

She slipped out of his grasp and swam to the shore.

He watched her. "You surrender?"

Nikki stepped out of the water and then took off her bikini bottoms and waved them in the air. "Does this look like surrender?"

"Come here."

She dropped her bikini bottoms on the ground and slowly walked toward him, the silky water rising up to meet her. "Are you going to let me catch you?"

Lucian let her catch him and a lot more. His mouth met hers and soon his body was on top of hers, and she felt the cool, wet sand pressed against her back, the waves cascading over their bodies. She could smell the sea on him and his own earthy scent. And as his roaming hands embraced her, she felt intoxicated by her own need for him, her need to be with him.

"Let me do the other rooms," Nikki breathed.

Lucian gave a hoarse laugh of surprise. "I knew there was a price."

"You can afford it." She slid her hand down his back, curving into him.

"Can I?"

"I want you to trust me. I have lots of ideas."

His hand scaled down her chest. "Let me see what you do with the room first."

"If you like it, will you concede?"

His eyes gleamed with humor. "I can lie."

"You won't."

"You sound confident about that."

"You're an honest man. And I know you're going to like it."

"Fine. Now stop talking." He silenced her with a deep, slow kiss.

"So you've forgiven me?" Nikki asked when he drew away.

"I don't care what you think of me anymore," Lucian said in a ragged whisper. "I want you too much. When I saw you standing there naked as the soft rays of the setting sun touched your skin, I knew nothing else mattered. I don't care what anyone says or thinks. I know what I am and I know what I look like. I know it's revolting, and you can scream in terror if you want to, but it won't stop me tonight."

"I won't scream," Nikki said, letting her fingers caress the raised flesh on his back. "The only sounds I'll make will be of exquisite pleasure." She spread her legs, making entrance easy. "Do I have to wait?"

His answer was eloquent enough for both of them. And together they were filled with a passionate completeness. They no longer felt like bodies, but entwined souls.

"Call me a greedy bastard," Lucian said in an almost savage voice. "Because I want to feel every inch of you."

"Only if you'll let me do the same," Nikki said, showering him with kisses. "Lucian, you are magnificent. In your arms I feel like a queen. No, don't let go. Hold me tight." She wrapped her legs around him. "Do you feel like a man now?"

"I need some more persuasion."

"With pleasure."

They made love until they were both exhausted and the sun had disappeared. Finally they pulled away, and Lucian stared up at the sky, feeling as if he could float up to the stars. "You should go to bed."

"Would you like to join me?"

Yes, but he didn't want to have her see him struggle into his trunks and limp his way back to the house. He wanted her to remember him as he was now: in the water, where he could carry her and hold her, where he seemed strong. On land all that was lost. "Another time."

Nikki put on her robe, then bent down to kiss him. "Good night. Dream of me."

He closed his eyes. "I already do," he said, and he heard her laughter as she walked away.

She wouldn't sleep that night. Nikki casually wandered up the stairs, heading toward her bedroom as if in a dream. That was when she heard it: the soft sound of a harp playing. Beautiful, haunting music. Where was it coming from? She tiptoed down the hall and heard it coming from Callia's room, but saw no lights. She slowly opened the door.

"You hear it, too?" Callia said, wide awake in her bed, with her knees drawn to her chest. Pauline sat next to her.

Nikki turned on the lights. The music abruptly stopped.

"You heard it," Callia said. "Please tell me you heard it."

"Yes, I heard something."

"So I'm not crazy."

"I told you you're not," Nikki said, searching the room for where the sound could have come from.

Callia held her knees tighter. "It was her favorite tune."

"I'm sure it's just a recording someone was listening to and it drifted through the vents."

Callia shook her head. "Everyone's asleep and no one listens to that kind of music here."

After looking around, Nikki gave up her search and sat on the bed. "Well, it's gone now."

Callia studied her for a moment, then began to smile. "Your hair's wet. Did you go swimming with Uncle Lucian?"

That and more. "Yes."

"So he'll let you stay longer?"

"A few more days and you'll get to see the room, and then we'll see what he says."

"It looks like a big project."

"It is."

Callia slipped under the covers. "I hope he'll like it."

Nikki turned out the lights. "Me too."

Chapter 14

"Don't be nervous," Dante said as he stood beside Nikki in front of the closed door.

Basilio, Callia and Kay waited with them. Lucian hadn't arrived yet.

"I'm not nervous," she said.

He glanced at her clenched fists.

She noticed his look and relaxed her hands. "Okay, maybe a little nervous."

"You have nothing to worry about. You've done an outstanding job."

"With your help." She hadn't seen Lucian all day. He'd had to travel for business. She hadn't seen him since their late-night beach escapade. This wasn't how she wanted to see him again.

Basilio frowned, suspicious. "What are you two whispering about?"

Dante shot him a look but remained silent.

Nikki took Basilio's arm, wanting to ease the tension she felt between the two men. "We're trying to imagine Lucian's reaction."

Basilio glanced at his watch. "And where's Lucian, anyway?"

"I'm right here."

Nikki fought to keep her composure, not sure which Lucian she would see. He would always be the man she loved, but would he pretend that the night on the beach never happened? Would she just be another employee again? She didn't expect a public display of his affection, but would he offer her even a crumb of acknowledgment that she meant more to him? Did she mean anything to him?

His eyes caught and held hers. "Don't look so nervous."

"That's what I've been telling her," Dante said.

"You should listen to him." Lucian gave her a soft smile and she felt herself relax under the warm glow of his gaze.

"Dante, show them in," she said.

Dante made a sweeping gesture. "Prepare to be amazed."

"What is this?" Basilio said with a smirk. "The circus?"

Callia sent him a cutting glance. "If this were the circus, you'd be the dancing monkey."

"Mind your manners," Kay said.

"She doesn't have any to mind," Basilio said.

"Quiet, children," Lucian said. "Continue, Dante."

Dante opened the door and revealed a room that left all of them speechless. From left to right, there were no longer walls, but what seemed like sheets of sculptured glass. A series of floor-to-ceiling Japanese screen doors had been constructed and put together, creating what looked like a continuous wall, but each one could be independently opened or shut, allowing in only as much scenery as one desired. Soft, muted colors of the sea were intertwined with splashes of bold colors, including several handblown emerald-green standing lamps, bright red and yellow retrograde artist-like chairs, and two sumptuous, oversize, soft black leather sofas.

There was no artwork on the walls. Instead one of the wall panels turned out to be a water fountain, while another was an aquarium—sporting a wonderful collection of brightly colored rare specimens. No detail had been spared. Just as she had done with J.D. and Monica's house, Nikki had included a series of retractable skylights, which allowed for an array of exotic plants to be strategically placed throughout. The final touch had been added by the theatrical lighting expert Nikki had hired, a man who had been a pain to work with, but whose results were worth all the effort. A series of small- and medium-size spotlights was strategically placed to create whatever kind of ambience or atmosphere a person desired.

"You're a genius," Basilio said, stepping inside and slowly turning to see everything.

"It's wonderful," Callia said. "The way the light comes through is so amazing."

Kay stared, speechless.

"It's like nothing I've ever seen," Dante said. "Don't you think, Lucian?"

Lucian stood and tapped the head of his cane, saying nothing. His expression unreadable.

Nikki folded her arms, her anxiety rising again. Was it too much of a change? "If there's anything you want altered—"

Lucian lowered his head. "Leave us."

"Come on, Lucian. You have to admit that this is amazing," Basilio said.

"Uncle, please," Callia added.

Lucian raised his head, his tone a command. "I said leave us." He shook his head. "Not a word, Dante."

Dante sighed and closed his mouth and reluctantly followed everyone out the door.

Once they were gone, Lucian said, "Come here."

Nikki walked over to him. "Yes?"

His eyes studied her in amazement. "I'm still trying to figure out if you're a goddess or a sorceress." He reached out and pulled her to him, his mouth covering hers with a wild passion. "I've been wanting to do that for days."

"And I've been wanting you to. I have been thinking of you since you left. I thought—"

"That I'd forget you? I could never forget you," he said with feeling. He looked around, amazed. "How did you do it?"

Nikki laughed, her heart feeling as if it could burst. "That's my secret."

"I want you to redesign every room in this house."

"That's a lot of rooms."

"I'll make it worth your while."

"I know, but I still have business back in New York. I only planned on being away three months, tops."

"Done. Do whatever you want in that time." He snapped his fingers. "I know. Redo all the rooms on this floor, and once you're done, I'll host a big party in your honor."

"A party for me?"

"Yes. That will give me a chance to surprise you."

"I'll do it."

They heard a tiny yelp of joy behind the door.

"Do you think they're listening in?" Nikki said, lowering her voice.

"I know they are. Only Dante will pretend he's not."

"Do you think they know about us?"

"If they don't, they will." Lucian opened the door and saw Callia playing with Pauline, while Kay looked at Basilio straightening his shirt and Dante pretended to be on the phone. Lucian walked over to him and took the phone. "It's upside down."

"I knew that," Dante said, taking it back.

"Right," Lucian said, repressing a smile. "I doubt this will be news to you. But Nikki is staying for a few more months to design the other rooms on this floor."

"Can she do mine, too?" Callia asked.

Lucian looked at her and Nikki nodded. "Yes."

"And what about the party?" Callia said. "Can I come too?"

Lucian looked blank. "What party?"

"I thought you said you'd host a party—" She stopped, realizing her mistake.

Basilio shook his head. "You goof."

"That's okay," Lucian said. "Yes, you can come."

"This is great!" Callia said. "We haven't had a party here since…for a long time."

"I'll make sure everything's in order," Dante said.

"I can always trust you." Lucian tapped his cane. "I feel like going somewhere."

Nikki looked at him in dismay. "But you just came back."

"You want to go to the beach?" Callia said.

"The yacht," Basilio guessed.

Lucian shook his head. "No. Turkey." He turned to

Nikki. "Go pack." He looked at Callia's eager face and smiled. "Yes, and you, too."

"And Dante?" Callia said, hopeful.

"I have to stay and look after the house," Dante said.

"We have guards for that." Callia turned to Lucian. "Uncle, please convince him to come. He used to before."

"But now you have Basilio," Dante said.

"Together we'll have lots of fun," Basilio said with a smile.

It clearly wasn't the replacement she wanted, but Callia left without arguing. Basilio and Kay followed.

"You should come and relax," Nikki said, looking at Dante. "You worked as hard as I did."

"Thanks, but no."

Nikki shrugged, then went to her room to pack.

Dante watched her go, then said in low tones, "Do you think it's wise to keep her here?"

"I don't care about being wise," Lucian replied. "I want her here."

"So do I, but—"

"I'll keep her safe. Everything's in place. Nothing will happen. I have my eyes on my enemy."

"But your weakness is evident, too."

"Nikki isn't my weakness." Lucian lifted his cane and shook it. "She makes me feel strong. She makes life sweeter and no one will steal that away from me again."

And for the next couple of weeks Lucian took Nikki on a wild adventure. Although Nikki had worked for many wealthy, powerful men over the years, she had never been the object of their desire. Gratitude, yes. Lust, no. And Lucian showed her how much she had missed. While Basilio, Callia and Kay had their own scheduled holiday, Lucian made his own arrangements for the two of them. But while Nikki thought she and Lucian would be alone, she was grossly mistaken. Wherever they went, a small entourage of assistants appeared out of nowhere, providing them with every element of luxury they needed. Fortunately, they disappeared just as quickly, giving the two of them ample time alone.

He flew them to Kusadasi, Turkey—where they continued their romantic interlude and visited several of the Greek islands. On the island of Crete, in a small village called Chania, Nikki indulged her fantasy and met with a famous local architect—who spent most of the morning discussing the history of the charming Venetian streets and the old Venetian harbor, which featured a sixteenth-century Venetian lighthouse. She didn't know how he arranged it, but that night, Lucian made arrangements for the two of them to enjoy a private outdoor dining experience on the grounds of the lighthouse. And prior to their meeting Nikki found a beautiful shimmering gown, a pair of shoes, and an expensive set of jewelry in her room, just in time for the occasion. When Lucian saw her that night, not only did they dine well, but just as he had done in the water off of his island, he indulged in his favorite pastime of undressing her layer by layer, and they made love in their hotel room until early morning.

In the city of Rethymnon, they enjoyed exploring the old quarter, because it was one of the best places to see Venetian and Turkish influences. Nikki especially loved the time she spent visiting some of the local markets and collecting a large number of handmade leather goods and pottery. Before long, she grew used to the help, which always appeared when she needed it. They packed the items she had collected and had them shipped back to the mansion.

On yet another night, Lucian treated Nikki to a horse-drawn carriage ride, which ended with a picnic on the beach—in an enormous tent, with all the accoutrements of wealth, including fine china and upholstered chairs. Even a chandelier was erected so that they were comfortable. Following a sumptuous dinner, the waitstaff disappeared, while the two of them lost themselves in each other's arms.

One of the last trips Lucian took her on was a tour of Istanbul by night. They flew there directly, where he had a reservation for them at one of the most exclusive international clubs in the area. There they were treated to a four-course dinner, followed by a night of belly dancers and a fleet of talented local musicians.

"Tomorrow we are going to visit my favorite place, before we have to return home," Lucian said. Nikki wasn't sure there were any places left that they hadn't been. But the next morning they traveled by private yacht to Santorini—a volcanic island. Upon arrival, they were met by a very cheerful individual who had a pair of scooters waiting for them. After donning their traveling gear—riding helmet and gloves—the two took off exploring the hills and the valleys and taking in the exquisite views they came upon. In one of the small towns, Lucian had arranged for a very special treat: to have Nikki's portrait done by a local watercolorist. Not only was he quick—it took less than an hour—but with a little prodding from her, he agreed to do a quick study of the two of them.

"Make her look like the goddess Artemis," Lucian instructed.

"And you?" the painter asked.

"I'll be Hephaestus."

"No, he won't," Nikki said.

Lucian looked at her, surprised. "Why not?"

"Because he was the crippled god of fire and was married to the adulterous Aphrodite and thrown off Mount Olympus because he was so ugly."

Lucian shrugged. "Sounds about right to me. We'll just keep Alana out of the picture." He nodded to the painter. "Go ahead."

"No," Nikki said. "He's Poseidon." She looked at Lucian. "At first I compared you to Hades, but I've gotten to know you better. Now smile."

Lucian lifted his chin and stared at the painter. "Gods don't smile."

The painter took that as his cue and went to work. He was an excellent craftsman. When leaving, Nikki made sure the rolled canvas was safely secured with her other belongings. It was one souvenir she knew she would treasure.

But one of the things they enjoyed most about visiting Santorini was seeing why it was famous, namely for the volcanic origin of the famous black pebble beach of Kamari. Days and nights became a dizzying array of places to see, new foods to enjoy, exquisite clothes and expensive jewelry to wear, and Nikki felt she was living a dream. No man had ever indulged her to this extent—and she knew that Benjamin would never be able to equal what Lucian could provide. And she discovered she liked—no, loved—it. She reveled in Lucian's attention, his kindness, his money, but mostly his affection.

From the many pictures Callia took, it was clearly obvious that she already knew what it was like being spoiled by her uncle. Although Callia, Kay and Basilio did some things with Lucian and Nikki, Callia was more than happy to have an open bank account and Kay to herself. While she wasn't yet ready to wear makeup, she loved shopping—for anything—and spent most of her time discovering the newest fashions and accessories the young women were wearing in the area.

One day Nikki persuaded Kay to let her take Callia shopping. They decided to go shopping for bathing suits. Nikki quickly found one to replace the one Lucian had tossed. Then she helped Callia select one. When the young woman tried on one that was essentially only two strings tied together, Nikki could only stare.

"Do you think Dante would like this?" Callia said, showing off her budding figure.

"I think he'd have a heart attack. And your uncle would never let you leave your room. Let's find something more suitable."

After finally settling on a more age-appropriate bathing suit, they went shopping for gifts for Kay, Lucian, Dante and Basilio. Once back in their hotel suite, Callia looked at her bulging bags, satisfied.

"Good, I have gifts for everyone."

"Not everyone."

"Who did I miss?"

"Your mother. She's arriving next week."

Callia fell face-forward on her bed and groaned.

"It won't be hard to pick up something for her."

Callia mumbled into the sheets, "It doesn't matter what I get her. She won't like it."

"She will."

Callia sent Nikki a flat look. "When you meet her, you'll see."

Later that day they quickly bought Callia's mother a

suitable gift from the hotel shop, and then they all returned to the island. That night Lucian invited Nikki to his bedroom for the first time. When she stepped inside, she was less than enthused.

"You don't like it?" he said, reading her face.

"Do you expect me to make love in a cave?"

"It's not a cave."

"It's close. It's so dark. There's nothing to catch the light. How do you change without a mirror?"

"I have a mirror." He opened his closet door. "See?"

"But there's no softness. I'm surprised you can sleep in here."

"Well, I don't plan to sleep in here right now."

"You should let me work on redesigning this room."

He drew her close and kissed her. "I'd prefer you work on me."

"You're harder to redesign."

"Tonight I'll make it easy," he said, then kissed her again, making her forget about the room altogether.

Chapter 15

"She's arrived," Dante told Nikki as she came out of her room. For the last several days the household had been preparing for Callia's mother's visit. "She's just touched down."

"Okay. I'll head down to the conservatory." She saw the servants rushing back and forth to make sure that everything was in order. "Is all this really necessary?"

"Yes," Dante said in a terse voice, leaving no room for further comment. "Excuse me."

Nikki walked into the conservatory, where Callia sat with a frown. "Your mother has arrived on the island."

"I know," she said in a sullen voice.

"Try to be happy to see her."

"I am trying."

"Try with a smile."

Callia pulled her face into a comical imitation of a smile.

Nikki laughed and went over to the window, and her mouth nearly fell open. "You've got to be kidding me," she mumbled as she saw Callia's mother being carried up the path to the mansion in an ancient Turkish litter. She knew that the woman couldn't walk, but she hadn't expected this.

Callia came and stood beside her. "Mom likes everything to be a production. She knows Uncle Lucian can afford it."

"I wish I had a camera."

"Quick! She's coming."

Nikki grabbed her measuring tape and went to a far wall, while Callia sat by Kay and waited for her mother's entrance.

They heard her booming voice first, her Northeast American accent. "The flight in the helicopter was bumpier than I would have liked, Lucian."

"I'm sorry," he said. "I'll make sure your return flight is smoother."

"Already thinking of sending me away?"

"Callia is waiting for you," Lucian said, avoiding the question.

Moments later the doors opened and Wanda Matthews appeared. She looked like the kind of woman who'd smell like old cigarettes and stale perfume, although she indulged in neither. Her hair was overdone, as was her makeup, but her clothes were exquisite. She had a face that could be called attractive, but years of bitterness had marred its surface with harsh lines and tight, dry skin. The men set her on a chaise surrounded by live exotic flowers and a host of silk cushions. A wheelchair sat discreetly over in the corner. For now Wanda was situated like a queen.

She smiled at her helpers, then looked at Callia and

held out her arms. "Karen! Aren't you going to give your mother a kiss?"

Callia walked over to her mother and gave her a perfunctory kiss on the forehead. "My name is Callia Kontos."

"Your name is Karen Matthews and you were born in White Plains, New York. I should know." She tapped her chest. "I was there."

Callia sat down, with Pauline in her lap.

"What's that?" Wanda said, looking at the kitten.

"Her name is Pauline."

"I know Lucian likes those things, but I didn't think he'd get you one, too."

"She keeps me company."

"Animals carry diseases."

"She doesn't."

Wanda looked around the room. "Is there anything to drink around here?"

Callia gestured to the tray next to Wanda, just within arm's reach. "There's lemonade."

Wanda smiled. "I meant a proper drink, honey."

"That will have to do." Callia stood and poured her mother a glass. "It's very good. Cook made it especially for you." She handed it to her.

Wanda reluctantly took it and had a sip. "Sweet and cool. But doesn't quite hit the spot. Honey, you can finish it for me. Mom needs an adult drink." She glanced at Nikki and snapped her fingers. "You. I'd like a drink."

Callia set the glass down on the tray. "She doesn't do that."

"Then what does she do?"

"She's an interior designer."

Wanda looked at Nikki with more interest. "Is that right?"

"Mom, please just take the drink. It will make you feel better." Callia returned to her seat and slunk down.

Wanda noticed and frowned. "Sit up straight. When will you return to boarding school?"

"I'm doing well in my studies here."

"Still having nightmares?"

"I'm having one right now."

"Callia," Kay warned.

Wanda stiffened. "I shouldn't have let you stay with him. What lies has he told you about me, Karen?"

"Callia," she quietly corrected.

"Karen," Wanda repeated. "You're my daughter, not his, and I named you. He took my husband, but I won't let him take you from me. I only have you here so that he can give you the best, and I can't take care of you the way I'd like to. Why won't you understand that?" Wanda said, then dissolved into tears.

Callia took out a handkerchief as if she'd done this so many times before and handed it to her mother.

Wanda took it and wiped her eyes. "Oh, I wish your father were here. He was such a good man. Lucian stole him away from you before you ever got a chance to know him."

"No, Uncle Lucian talks about Daddy lots of times. He tells me about the fun they had at Cambridge and their travels together."

"I bet you wished I died in that crash instead of him."

Callia stroked Pauline. "I bet sometimes you do, too."

Kay jumped to her feet. "Go to your room."

"No," Wanda said. "She's right."

"Would you like something to eat, Ms. Matthews?" Kay said, trying to smooth over the awkward moment.

"No." She touched her forehead with the back of her hand. "It's been a long journey. I think I'll take a nap. Will anyone mind if I just close my eyes here?"

"No, that's fine. Come, Callia," Kay said.

Kay and Callia left the room, and Nikki closed the measuring tape, ready to follow.

"No," Wanda said as Nikki headed for the door. "You don't need to leave, too."

"But if you'd like to rest," Nikki said, sending a look of longing at the door. She just wanted to leave. "I'd hate to disturb you."

"You won't. Just stay a few minutes. Sit down."

Nikki did so, knowing Wanda was the type of woman who was used to giving orders. She waited.

"I've used a designer before. It was a good experience."

"I'm glad."

"She got to know a lot about me. That happens when you work closely with someone."

"Yes," Nikki said, not sure what Wanda's point was.

"What have you learned about Lucian?"

"No more than most."

"I doubt that." Wanda studied her. "You're just his type. He likes the brown skins and the dark ones. James told me they were his weakness. You have beautiful skin. What do you do to keep that complexion?"

"Ms. Matthews, I'm flattered, but I just work here."

Wanda smiled. "No, you don't. I see the way that Karen and Kay look at you. And you don't act like staff. You act as if you belong here. As if you're mistress of this place."

"I can assure you that I'm not."

"I never met Alana, but Karen showed me a picture. An extraordinary woman. I wasn't surprised Lucian fell so hard."

"Did Callia like her?" Nikki couldn't help but ask.

"Karen doesn't talk to me about things like that. I suppose she did like her. She seemed in awe of her. Everyone was." Wanda looked around the room. "I haven't been in this house in years. They replaced a lot and changed things, but so many memories remain, that makes it seem exactly the same."

Nikki stood. "I really have to go. Excuse me."

"Yes," Wanda said, closing her eyes. "I really need to rest."

Nikki hurried out of the room and closed the door, then rested against it in relief.

"Is she still in there?" Lucian asked, coming out of another room.

"Yes. She's taking a nap."

"Thank God." He ran a hand down his face. "That gives us some breathing room."

"She's a handful," Nikki said, choosing her words carefully.

"She's a dreadful woman."

"I find her a little sad."

"I begged James not to marry her, but he was in love and I couldn't stop him. I really do believe that love is a curse."

Nikki shook her head. "No, love is like water. It's neutral. It's what people add to it that changes its complexion. They allow it to blind them or help them to see clearly. It can poison them or heal them. On its own, love, like water, is pure and nourishes. It's what we need to live."

Lucian's eyes clung to hers and his voice deepened. "I never thought of it that way before."

"Lucian?" Wanda called. "Is that you out there?"

Lucian rolled his eyes and lowered his voice. "I thought you said she was asleep."

Nikki shrugged. "She seemed to be when I left her."

"Lucian?" Wanda repeated.

"Should I lie?"

Nikki bit her lip, trying not to laugh. "It won't help."

"Lucian?" Wanda called again, louder this time.

"Yes, I'm coming," he said, kissing Nikki quickly before going into the room.

Chapter 16

"I'd love a drink," Wanda said as Lucian took a seat.

"There's a glass right beside you."

"It's not the same."

Lucian sat back, making no move to fulfill her request. "But you didn't call me in here for that. What do you really want?"

"I need more money."

"How much more?"

"What does it matter? You can afford it."

"I can afford a lot of things. That doesn't mean I'll spend my money on them."

"My husband helped you make some of that money."

"And you're benefiting from it, too, and you will for the rest of your life."

"It's not enough."

Lucian leaned forward. "What do you need the extra money for?"

"That's my business."

"Then the answer's no."

"You owe me, Lucian. You took my husband and made my daughter think she belongs to some half-Greek bastard."

"Do you want to take her back?" he said in a soft challenge.

"You know I can't."

"I know you won't. I know that James's death was partly a relief to you, because you didn't like being the wife of a high-powered executive. You envied his ambition. You hated anything that competed with his attention for you. Even Callia."

"Her name is Karen!"

"No, it's not. You know that James let me give her her middle name and that's the one she prefers. Is that all?"

Wanda looked at him, suddenly helpless. "Lucian, I did love him. And I do love her. It's all just been too much for me. Just help me with fifty thousand. That's all. That's pocket change to you."

He glanced at the barely touched glass of lemonade. "When you stop drinking, I'll consider your request."

"I just drink to calm my nerves."

"I doubt you feel them anymore. You've been numbing yourself for years." Lucian stood and sat down on the chaise beside her. "When Callia was young, you handled yourself better and your addiction was less…" he searched for words "…pronounced. Now you're slipping and Callia's older. You can't hide it anymore."

"I'm not a strong woman, Lucian. Don't force me to pretend to be."

"You're strong enough."

"I'm afraid."

"I'll pay for treatment."

Wanda briefly closed her eyes. "You've always made it so hard for me to hate you." She looked at him. "And I've wanted to."

"Let's start again." He held out his hand. "To new beginnings."

She shook his hand. "Yes." Her mouth curved into a weary grin. "I guess it would be inappropriate to celebrate with a drink?"

"Yes, but I think we can find something else."

After what seemed like a reasonable length of time, Lucian treated her to a delightful nonalcoholic drink that suited her taste, and on the last day of her stay the chef created a sumptuous feast featuring many prized local Mediterranean dishes, which Wanda indulged in before she pulled Callia aside.

"You've grown so much."

"Yes."

"For your birthday I'd like to give you something you've always wanted."

"What?"

"I'm going to give up custody and allow Lucian to legally adopt you."

Callia stared at her mother, in shock, and then hugged her. It was the first truly affectionate gesture she'd made in years, and tears came to Wanda's eyes. She wiped them away.

"I'd still like you to visit every now and then."

"I will."

After Wanda's departure, things quickly returned to normal. Nikki continued her work designing the other four rooms. She also helped design Callia's bedroom, as promised. Nikki didn't do as dramatic a makeover as she had done with the other rooms, because the layout and design were great—there were plenty of windows, a window seat and ample closet space. What the room desperately needed was a new coat of paint, colorful drapery and modern furniture. She did take her time, however, with the bed. Instead of the enormous bed suited more for a giant that Callia had previously, Nikki ordered a queen-size poster bed with a princess canopy. She also had a special set of sheets, pillowcases and a comforter designed with silhouettes of Pauline on them. When she showed Callia the transformed room, she was overcome. It was exactly what she needed, something more sophisticated and adult. While she loved her new bed and customized bedding, she definitely loved the three-way mirror Nikki had installed, fashioned after one she'd seen in her sister's closet when she used to model.

She hugged Nikki. "All my dreams are coming true. Uncle Lucian will be my legal guardian and now I have this beautiful room. I won't have nightmares in here. Thank you for everything."

"You're welcome."

"Would you like to be a mom someday?"

"I've never really thought about it," Nikki said, unprepared for the question. "Probably."

"You'd probably want your own kids, right? Not someone else's."

"My heart is open to loving many children. Family comes in all forms."

"I'd love to have a real mom someday."

"You do have a real mom. She's not perfect, but she's yours and you have to accept that. She does love you."

"I think you'd make a great mom."

"Thank you."

"And an aunt."

"I think so."

"I make a great niece."

"I know you do. Your uncle Lucian tells me so."

"I'm so glad you're here. You make the place happy, unlike…"

"Alana?"

"No, she could make the place happy, too, when she was in a good mood."

"Did you like her?"

Callia shrugged. "She was nice to me. But she was always nice to people she liked, but if she didn't like you, then she was mean. Especially to servants. But she never let Uncle Lucian see that, because she knew that would make him angry."

"And the servants never told him?"

"They didn't dare. Alana could be scary. I didn't mind her as much until her uncle and cousin came to visit. I didn't like them much, because they ignored me and always kept their doors closed, like they were hiding something. Uncle didn't notice, because he thinks family's important and felt that Alana's family would soon be his own."

"He has a point. Family is important."

"Maybe."

"Don't you miss being around other children?"

"No." She took Nikki's hand. "Come on. Let's show the others what you did to my room."

Lucian, Dante, Kay and Basilio were as impressed as when Nikki revealed her other completed projects. Lucian and Dante immediately started to make arrangements for the party and prepare for the guests who would come.

* * *

"What are you doing here?" Iona said, surprised when she opened her bedroom door and saw Basilio.

"I wanted to see you. Because we're preparing for the party and extra guests, the villas won't be as safe as before. Someone may see us."

"You *never* come down here."

"But I'm here now. Are you going to let me in?"

"Give me a minute," she said, half closing the door. He heard her shift something and caught a glance of a lace dress before she opened the door wider to let him in.

"You seem anxious," Basilio said.

"I have a lot of work to do, that's all." She kissed him. "But I know that you can help me relax."

And for the next hour he did just that.

"I can't believe that Nikki woman has managed to stay on this long," Iona said as she and Basilio lay in bed.

"Yes. She's cast a spell over him."

"Just like the other one."

"No, she's different."

"She's dangerous to us."

"No, she's not. She hasn't said anything."

"Yet."

"I trust her. She calms Callia. She hasn't screamed out in weeks. Lucian even told me that Nikki heard the strange music Callia used to go on about, so that shows she wasn't making it up. We may not need Kay any longer."

"But poor Kay still needs the money."

"Lucian will give her another position. Don't worry. He'll take care of her."

* * *

"I got the invitation from Lucian!" Monica said to Nikki over the phone. "J.D. says Lucian hardly ever throws parties, even small ones. How did you manage it?"

"I didn't," Nikki said. "It's this place. You feel wonderful here and want to share it."

"You like him, don't you?"

"I love him."

Monica was silent a moment. "Does he know?"

"No, I'm not sure he feels the same. He's grateful, but I'm not sure it goes further than that."

"You have enough time to change his mind."

"Well, we'll see. Are you coming?"

"Oh, yes. J.D. and I have already put it on the schedule. The trip will be too grueling for the little ones, so we're hiring a babysitter for the week."

"I can't wait to see you."

"Me, too, and I can't wait to see what you've done."

"To the house?"

"No," Monica said with a laugh. "To Lucian."

Nikki returned to her room after a relaxing walk and saw a large dress box on her bed. Lucian was truly spoiling her, but she'd quickly gotten used to his extravagant surprises. He was so generous when it came to gifts. She smiled as she opened the box, then gasped at what was inside. It was a full-length, dark blue, off-the-shoulder lace dress, made entirely by hand. Underneath the intricate design of tiny seashells was a soft, off-gray, almost transparent silk lining, with a thigh-high slit on one side. Nikki knew she'd be a knockout wearing it.

She went to her mirror and held the dress up against her. It was the perfect outfit for the party.

She rushed downstairs and found Lucian in his study. She wrapped her arms around him and kissed him.

He smiled, pleased. "What's that for?"

"You know."

"Are you ready for this weekend?"

"Oh, definitely."

"What will you wear?"

She grinned at his teasing. "You know."

He raised a brow. "Really?"

"Yes, and I'm going to look fabulous."

"I can't wait."

Chapter 17

Monica and J.D. arrived two days before the party. Lucian had designated a private villa for them nearby, but they preferred staying at the mansion. When the sisters saw each other, they hugged as if they hadn't seen each other in years. J.D. went with Lucian into his private sitting room, while Nikki helped her sister unpack.

"You're glowing," Monica said.

"It's the island."

"It's Lucian. Give the man some credit." Monica sat on the bed. "Now, tell me everything."

And she did. She shared about Callia's dreams, Basilio's secret and Iona.

"Wow, you *have* been busy," Monica said.

"So you don't think—"

"That Lucian could be a murderer?" Monica interrupted. "Absolutely not."

"How about Basilio?"

"I don't know him well enough to make an opinion, but Lucian's a smart man. He knows who he can trust."

"He made the wrong choice once."

"That means he won't again." Monica patted her sister's hand. "Don't worry."

"You're right," Nikki said, feeling better. If her sister didn't worry, she wouldn't, either. "The last couple of months have been wonderful, so I'm sure it's all nothing."

"I know the party will take your mind off of it."

J.D. popped his head in. "Anyone want to go for a swim?"

Moments later they were all settled on the beach. J.D. lifted Monica in his arms and spun her around, making her laugh. Nikki caught Lucian watching them. She wanted to tell him that she didn't care that he could never do that with her, that he was strong in other ways.

"They're like young lovers again," he said.

"Yes," Nikki replied. But she didn't want him thinking of them. Or comparing his skin to J.D.'s unblemished skin. She crawled onto his lap and rested her head in the curve of his neck. "Hold me."

He did, kissing the top of her head and stroking her back. "Sometimes I wish—"

"I love you."

His hand stopped. "What?"

She looked up at him. "I love you." She brushed her lips against his, then laid her head back down. "So you don't need to wish anymore."

He didn't say another word, but held her tighter, as if afraid of letting her go.

She loved him. Him. Lucian Kontos. Not his money or reputation, but him—the man. As he was. Lucian sat in his study, stunned. He held up his fist. *I will defeat you, Alana, and reclaim all that you stole from me.* One day he'd be able to carry Nikki to bed. He'd be able to join her on her morning jogs down by the beach. One day he'd walk beside her without a cane. The doctors and specialists said the damage was irreversible and that nothing could be done, that he'd always need to use a cane. But he'd prove them wrong.

He stood and set his cane aside. He took a deep breath and made his way to the door. His limp was marked but he made slow progress, but after a couple steps his leg gave way. He scrambled to catch himself on the couch but missed and collapsed on the floor with a thud.

Dante raced into the room and stared down at him. "Are you okay?"

"I'm fine," Lucian said, embarrassed.

Dante glanced up and noticed where Lucian had left his cane. "She doesn't care, you know."

"I care, dammit," he said in a harsh tone.

Dante retrieved the cane and handed it to him. "Then I feel sorry for you."

Lucian snatched the cane and slowly stood. "She deserves—"

"A man who loves her."

"What?"

"Lucian, your leg may never recover, but is your heart irreparable, too?"

Lucian groaned, then playfully punched Dante on the chin. "I should fire you. You take too many liberties for a butler."

"You can't fire me. I know all your secrets."

Lucian sobered. "Yes, you do."

"And I will keep every last one."

Basilio knocked on the door, then entered. "Dante," he said in a cold tone, "you're needed in the kitchen."

Dante nodded, then left.

Lucian walked to his desk and sat. "You should watch your tone with him."

"Why? He's just a servant."

"Nobody's just anything. Everyone deserves respect—especially those who serve you."

"I know he's your favorite."

"I also know I'm not the only one here who has a favorite."

Basilio shoved his hands in his pockets. "What do you mean? What have you heard?"

"I warned you about Iona."

"Did Nikki tell you—" He stopped when he saw his brother's face change.

Lucian slowly stood. "Did Nikki tell me what?"

"Nothing."

Lucian came from around the desk, his voice hard. "Did Nikki tell me what?" he repeated, demanding an answer.

"She misunderstood a conversation I was having with Iona, that's all. I may have scared her a little."

"She was terrified. You're the one who put those bruises on her arm? No wonder she didn't tell me. God, and I even suggested that she go to you."

"I didn't mean—"

Lucian raised his cane. "If you touch her again in anger, I will beat you with this stick until you beg for mercy. Am I clear?"

"Yes."

Lucian set his cane down. "You never touch a woman in anger."

Basilio hung his head. "I know."

"You did that night."

"I forgot."

"There are certain things that are dangerous to forget."

His head shot up. "I won't do it again. I promise."

Lucian rested against his desk. "Nikki kept your 'misunderstanding' to herself. It was Dante who told me."

Basilio frowned. "Dante is a gossip who should mind his own business."

"You *are* my business. There are certain things you don't know. Whatever you have with Iona, I want it to end. Or I will end it for you."

Basilio marched down the hall, wanting to punch something. His brother couldn't do this to him. He wouldn't let Lucian separate him from Iona. The woman he loved. Maybe she was right. He did let his brother watch him and baby him too much. Lucian had Nikki, who he paid to design his house. How was that different than him being with a maid? Iona made him happy. No, he would have her. He would do what she asked him, and then nothing and nobody could come between them.

"He knows," he told her that night, using the empty villa that had been prepared for Monica and J.D.

"What are you going to do?"

"I'm going to do what you asked me to. We'll wait until after the party and then we'll get married."

"Why not now?"

Basilio laughed at her eagerness. "I still have some things to do. I'll have to get a job and a new place for us. It won't be easy, but I'm ready."

"You think Lucian will cut you off?"

"Don't let it concern you."

"Family means too much to him. Sure, he'll be angry, but he'll forgive you. I think we should just do it now."

"No, and I told you why. I have to have a backup plan. I want to be able to take care of you myself."

"Hmm."

"Dante's been watching me and reporting back to Lucian. Can you believe it?"

"Yes, Lucian likes to control the lives of everyone around him."

Basilio pulled Iona close. "Well, he won't control me. And he won't control us anymore."

They made love that night and Basilio returned to the house early the next morning. The first person he saw was Dante, who was outside smoking. He walked over to him.

"I know what you're up to. You're trying to poison my brother against me."

"You sound like a jealous woman."

"How does it feel to be a babysitter?"

Dante blew smoke in his face. "How does it feel to be an imbecile?"

Basilio punched him in the face. Dante staggered back, then lunged at him, and the two men began to fight. The screams of the maids alerted J.D. and Lucian. J.D. jumped in and parted the men.

"What's going on?" he asked, looking at the two of them, bewildered.

Lucian didn't give them a chance to answer. Instead he said, "Study. Now."

Minutes later Basilio and Dante stood in his study and Lucian watched them with folded arms. "This is how you behave in front of my guests?"

"We apologize," Dante said.

"Don't apologize for me," Basilio retorted.

"It's too late for your mother to."

Basilio moved toward him, but Lucian whacked him on the arm with his cane. "Sit down and cool off."

Basilio rubbed his arm and sat.

Lucian looked at Dante. "You're overstepping."

"It's not the first time," Basilio said.

"And you're getting on my nerves," Lucian told him. "I don't even care why you did what you did. But I don't like disturbances. You don't need to like each other, but you have to respect each other. Basilio, if you have an issue with Dante's duties, you come to me. Dante, my brother is welcome here. Work on making him feel that way. Now shake hands."

Dante stepped forward and held out his hand. Basilio just looked at it.

"Shake hands or leave this house," Lucian said.

Basilio shook Dante's hand, then stormed out.

"Your brother has a temper," Dante said.

"Which you shouldn't have ignited. That was foolish."

"Yes, you're right."

"We can't afford errors in judgment like that. What happened?"

"He punched me," Dante said, taking out a cigarette.

"You've been punched before. If anything is distracting you, I can get—"

"I'm fine."

"You know better than that," Lucian said before Dante could light up.

Dante swore, surprised at his own carelessness. He never smoked in the house. "Sorry."

"Do you need a day off?"

"No, I can do my job. This won't happen again."

"Good. I count on that."

Chapter 18

The night of the party Monica helped Nikki dress with care. "You look stunning," she said.

"I feel wonderful."

"I'll go down first and then you follow a few minutes later. No one will be able to take their eyes off you." She kissed her sister on the cheek, then left.

Nikki checked her makeup and hair, then left the room. She took a deep breath before she descended the main stairs into the ballroom, which glimmered with lights and burst with extravagant floral decorations. She heard the sound of clinking glasses of champagne and soft music. As her sister had predicted, all eyes turned to look at Nikki. A quiet, uneasy hush quickly filled the room as all attention focused on her. Callia looked up at her and screamed.

The sound of shattering glass followed as Basilio

dropped his drink. Lucian stared at her with abject horror.

"It's her!" one person said.

"That's impossible. She's dead."

Nikki looked at her sister, who looked as confused as she felt. She forced a smile and grabbed a drink from a waiter standing nearby, who also appeared paralyzed.

Lucian pushed his way through the crowd and grabbed Nikki's hand. "Dear God, why are you wearing that dress?"

"What do you mean? You bought it for me."

He glanced at the dress, then turned away, as if the sight of it hurt his eyes. "I'd rather slice off my hand than give you a gift like that."

"You didn't put this dress in my bedroom?"

"Absolutely not. Go take it off."

Nikki blinked back tears, hearing the anguish in his voice. "Did I do something wrong?"

"No." He briefly covered his eyes with a trembling hand. "Just take it off."

"Tell me what I've done."

"You're wearing Alana's dress."

Blood drained from Nikki's face.

Lucian squeezed her hand. "Please just go and change. Everything will be okay."

Nikki didn't believe him. She'd inadvertently reminded him of a woman he'd fought to forget. She yanked her hand free from his and ran back upstairs and closed the door. She tore off the dress and tossed it on the floor. Someone had played a cruel joke on her. But who and why?

Someone knocked on the door, but she didn't answer.

Monica peeked her head in, then entered. "You have to come back downstairs."

"No, I don't. I can't face them—him."

"Nikki—"

"I'll probably give Callia more nightmares, and did you see Lucian's face? I might as well have started the fire all over again. All the happiness that was there is gone."

"He'll get over it. He knows it was a mistake."

Nikki shook her head. "Now every time he sees me, he'll see *her.*"

"It was just the dress that shocked everyone, not you. You're not her."

"Why would someone have done this?"

"I don't know."

"Callia said she's still here somehow."

"Then you have to fight her. Dupree women don't flee. We fight." Monica went to the closet. "Now, let's find you something to wear."

Nikki returned to the party dressed in a two-piece silk combo consisting of a sleeveless top trimmed with sequins and a straight, fitted A-line skirt with soft ruffles around the edges, looking less effusive than before.

"You look marvelous," Lucian said, pulling her into a dancer's embrace.

"I still feel awful."

"Then listen to the music," he said, his eyes piercing into hers. "And think only of me."

Nikki barely remembered the rest of the night, instead moving through it as if in a fog.

Once the party was over, she again disappeared into her room, but this time she started to pack. It was time to leave. She had nothing to keep her here now. She'd completed her job and she needed to start afresh somewhere else. And Lucian? What would happen with him? She didn't want to think about how painful it was to leave him, but could think of no other choice. She was pulling things from her closet when she heard the door open.

"What are you doing?" Lucian said.

"I thought I could leave with J.D. and Monica."

"Why?"

"It's a long trip."

He crossed the room and covered her hand. "I'm sorry about this evening, but you didn't do anything wrong."

"But—"

He pressed a finger against her lips. "You looked stunning tonight. I was honored to have you at my side."

Nikki lowered her face, but he lifted her chin, forcing her to face him. "Did you like the ice sculptures?"

"Yes."

"The champagne waterfall?"

"Yes."

"The music, the food, the flowers, the—"

"Lucian, I loved everything."

His gaze fell to her neck. "Good, because I did it all for you," he said as he slowly unzipped her skirt. "I'm glad you left this for me to do. I enjoy undressing you."

A tiny glow of renewed hope and joy grew inside her. His hands caressed her skin as he pushed her skirt down.

"It's not the same now," she said, her skin tingling.

"What's not the same?" Lucian said, removing her top.

"Every time you see me, you'll see her."

Lucian shook his head, his voice fierce. "No. Never," he said, then kissed her with a ferocity that both stunned and thrilled her. "You're all that I think or dream about, and that will never change."

She kissed him back, arching her body into his, wanting her love to wash over him. Tonight she wanted to erase Alana from his memory. She didn't want anyone or anything to come between them. Soon they were naked on the bed, their bodies moving in rhythmic harmony. Nikki held him close and gave her body completely to him, determined to make sure that she would be the only woman he ever remembered or wanted. She welcomed every part of him on her, over her, in her, swept away by her own intensive need for him.

He'd told Alana he loved her, but would he ever say that to her? Would he ever say he loved her? Did he love her? Did she need that from him? No. She had him now. That was what mattered. She opened her body even more to him, letting him fill her with an exploding ecstasy. No man had ever made her feel this way. And it had never been this way between them before. Somehow tonight their feelings were more intense, more urgent, deeper. But she wouldn't analyze it too much. All that mattered was that she wanted to kiss him, lick him, consume him—no part of his body was ugly to her. He was all man and he was wonderful, his scars a part of him she couldn't imagine him without. They were like medals—evidence of his survival, his courage, his heroism. She now wondered how she'd ever seen them as hideous before.

"You're so beautiful," she breathed.

Lucian laughed. "And how much have you had to drink tonight?"

"Not enough." She licked her lips. "I'm still thirsty."

"Want me to get you something?"

"No, you have all that I want," she said, then slid

down his body and wrapped her mouth around him and sucked until he climaxed.

Nikki wiped her mouth and winked. "That was fun."

"I'm getting a little hungry myself," Lucian said, then used his tongue to tease the sensitive part of her until she had to bite her fist to keep from screaming out. Soon teasing wasn't enough.

"Don't make me wait," she begged.

"Are you sure? I have a few more—"

Her fingers bit into his back. "I want you now."

Lucian didn't need any more coaxing and soon he was sending her senses spinning again. She wanted the moment to last forever.

"I wish you never had to let me go," she said, wishing she could be in his arms forever, because with him she didn't just feel safe or beautiful, but also strong and needed. She knew he needed her and that they were meant to be together.

"So do I," he said and he didn't let her go and they lay together, hardly able to move.

Nikki felt as if her body could melt into the mattress. She wanted to think of nothing but him, but the incident with the dress floated through her mind. She sighed.

"What's the sigh for?" Lucian asked.

"Someone made a fool of me tonight. I shouldn't have worn that dress."

Lucian hesitated, then said, "They didn't do it because of you. They did it because of me."

Nikki lifted her head to look at him. "What do you mean?"

His face became grave. "Someone knows my secret." He looked up at the ceiling. "Alana didn't start the fire." He turned to her. "I did."

Chapter 19

Nikki stared at Lucian, dumbfounded. "You? Why?"

"I didn't tell you the entire story of why I broke off my engagement with Alana. Yes, I did find her with one of my patrolmen, but only because Dante had given me a reason to return early from a trip and come home."

When he stopped, Nikki gently touched his arm. "What was it?"

"Dante had discovered Callia with a packet of powder she'd found hidden in one of the rooms, and learned it was cocaine. He then followed Alana's cousin and discovered a drop-off point."

"A drop off point?"

"Yes, Alana's cousin and uncle were smugglers and she was their leader. I learned that it wasn't just a small operation, but an international one, all based on my island. When I opened my home to her family, I never anticipated something like that. I didn't mind their long stays or question their comings and goings. I came home, and Dante and I discovered that they'd been smuggling and storing their stash in my home. Drugs, weapons, porn. My home had become a perverse den of depravity.

"I confronted her and that's what we argued about. She didn't want me to send them away, because they were in debt to a big-arms dealer who threatened to kill them if the delivery didn't go through. I didn't care and I sent them away. I heard her cousin's body was found floating on a beach in Portugal, and she likely blamed me and started her campaign of destruction. It was weeks later that I learned what she'd done with the money for the foundations, and she leaked stories to the press, determined to ruin my reputation.

"One day I stood looking at this place with rage. I was disgusted by my blindness. By then my reputation was destroyed, our engagement over, and I wanted everything gone. So I had Dante clear the house of all staff and we set it ablaze. I watched it burn with satisfaction, until everything changed," he said, remembering that night. He told Nikki what had happened.

Lucian had stood outside the house, watching the fire slowly take hold, while Dante stood beside him. It was over and he felt victorious. Then Lucian heard him gasp. He turned to him.

"What?"

"Dear God," Dante said, then made a sign of the cross.

"What is it?"

He pointed to the roof. "Look! Someone's in the house. Someone's still inside."

"That's impossible," Lucian said. Then he saw the figure, too. Alana. "What is she doing here?"

"Doesn't matter. There's nothing we can do."

Lucian quickly assessed the fire, then took off his jacket. "Yes, there is."

"You can't go in and get her."

"There's still time. She's trapped up there. I can't just let her die." He ran into the house and up the stairs to the roof, where he searched until he spotted her. "Alana."

She turned, her eyes wide and full of terror. "Why did you tell me to meet you here?"

He stopped. "I didn't."

"But I received your message."

"I didn't send you a message." He held out his hand. "Come quick. I know a way out."

She took a step toward the edge. "I thought once you knew about the baby, you'd forgive me."

"What baby?"

She touched her stomach. "Our baby. I know it's yours," she said, seeing the doubt on his face. "I've already had the tests done. Please don't desert us now."

Lucian waved his hand. "It doesn't matter now. Alana, come on. We have to get out of here."

"I thought you wanted me back," she said in a weak voice. "But now I know you don't want me at all."

"Alana, we can talk later."

She took another step back. "Promise you'll marry me."

Lucian grabbed her arm. "I'm not playing this game."

"It's not a game. I can't be shamed like this. What will my father think?"

"Your father, the murderer? You, the head of a smuggling ring? It doesn't matter."

"That was my cousin's idea."

"And you went along."

"I didn't know about it until too late. Lucian, please. I can make everything right if you'll only marry me."

"I'll take care of the baby. That's all I can promise."

"I do love you and there's something else you should know. There's—" Suddenly her eyes widened from something behind him. "No! Don't!"

Lucian spun around, but not fast enough. He felt a searing pain in his leg as a bullet passed through it, and heard three other shots. He grabbed Alana and dropped to the ground. The shooting abruptly stopped, and he cautiously looked up but didn't see anyone. Someone else was there, ready to kill him.

"Come, Alana. Let's get out of here." He looked at her and saw her sightless eyes staring back at him. Obviously the bullets meant for him had gotten her instead. He touched her face, wanting it to be a nightmare, wanting her to get up and tell him who she'd seen, but he knew the truth had died with her.

Lucian closed her eyes, then struggled to his feet and stumbled down the stairs, but his original escape route was blocked, so he went to his room and waited for death. Alana, and possibly his child, were dead— murdered. And someone wanted him dead, too, but he didn't care anymore. His life had no more meaning. He didn't care if he didn't escape. He sank into a chair and waited for death, until he heard a scream....

"That's when I heard Callia," Lucian told Nikki. "Someone killed Alana and wanted to kill me, but Callia was a true innocent and I needed to flush out who this person was. I won't deny that there was a cover-up. That's why I came up with the story of Alana starting the fire, to see if anyone would try to refute me. No one did. I rebuilt to see if anyone would slip up. No one did until tonight. That's when I knew my prey was close at hand and finally showing me their hand."

"Who?"

"I can't tell you until I'm absolutely certain. The less you know, the better, but I have a plan in place."

"You will be careful?"

"Yes." He took her hand. "I'm telling you all this because I want you to know the truth and why I'm willing to let you go."

"And if I stay?"

"It's too risky."

"You said you have a plan."

"I do, but what happened tonight has me worried." He shook his head. "But let's not talk anymore. Tonight we're safe."

Basilio felt sick. He remembered seeing the dress Nikki had worn to the party in Iona's room. He had to find out why. He went to her room and knocked on her door.

She opened it with a smile. "I'm not packed yet."

He pushed past her. "I'm not here for that."

She closed the door. "Then what are you here for?"

He glared at her. "To find out what you're up to."

"What do you mean?"

"That dress that Nikki wore tonight is the same one I saw in your room."

"It was given to me to hem."

"By whom?"

"I don't know," Iona said, annoyed by his question. "I found it hanging on my door with a printed message." She touched his face, her eyes searching his. "Don't you trust me, my love?"

He wanted to, but there were so many questions that

had slowly been growing in his mind and nagging him. Especially about the fire. "Of course I trust you, but—"

"But what?"

But why did she seem so interested in Nikki? What had she been doing on the night of the fire? How had she been able to assuage his guilt so well? How had she shown up at the same club he'd gone to on the mainland? No one else from the house had been there. It had been his biggest mistake and something he'd never told anyone. He'd left Callia alone in the hotel, thinking she was old enough to look after herself and would be safe as long as she stayed in her room.

That night he'd gone out for a drink at the local club he liked to frequent, where he'd met Iona. She came on to him and he was drunk enough to take her up on the offer. They returned to his hotel and went straight to bed. He didn't check on Callia in the next room. He just assumed everything was fine. He'd woken the next morning with Iona beside him and in good spirits. He ordered breakfast, and that was when he checked on Callia and realized she was gone.

He'd been so panicked, knowing what his brother would think, and Iona had calmed him down and told him what he should say. She stood by him and kept his secret, but now he wondered if she'd planned to be at the bar to meet him. But why? He'd once asked her how she ended up there and she'd said it was fate and he'd always taken her at her word. Now he wasn't so sure. But none of it made sense. Why would Iona do anything to hurt Callia? Or his brother?

"It's nothing," Basilio said, wondering if he really knew the woman he planned to marry.

"Are you sure you won't stay the night?" Iona said.

"It's been a long day. I'll just go to bed."

Iona looked disappointed but didn't reply.

Nikki woke to the sound of claws scratching at her door. The early morning light filtered through her room and she turned to see that Lucian was gone. The scratching continued. She got up and opened the door and looked down to see the kitten, Pauline, who meowed.

Nikki bent to pet her. "What's wrong?" she asked, then noticed blood on her paws. She stood and ran to Callia's room.

She swung open the door and found Callia's bed empty and Kay lying on the floor, with blood on the side of her head. Nikki knelt next to the woman and checked for a pulse. She breathed a sigh of relief when she found one.

"Kay?"

The woman moaned.

She gently shook her. "Kay, what happened?"

Kay groaned, then slowly got up. "God forgive me."

"Tell me what happened."

"This wasn't part of the agreement."

"What agreement?"

"Mr. Kontos will put me away for this."

Nikki shook her. "Where's Callia? Tell me what happened."

"My mother's sick, and I needed the money, so I took the job to look after Callia."

Nikki sighed, exasperated. "We all know that."

"What you don't know is that I was also paid to make her appear crazy. I didn't know who it was at first. It was just a voice on the phone who said that I could make extra money, and when it told me the amount, I couldn't resist. I placed a small speaker in Callia's room and filtered the harp music into her room, and at times I would play it and pretend not to hear it. I paid a woman to dress in Alana's clothes and go past the window or Callia's door, and I pretended not to see anything. When you came, I left the head scarf in the room, and that night, as Callia slept, I told her that you were really Alana, who'd come back. I also filtered subliminal messages."

"But why would you do that?"

"I didn't care at first. The money was too good, but then, when I discovered who was behind the voice and what she wanted, I didn't know what to do with someone so powerful."

"Powerful?"

"Yes, she was going to marry into the family and I knew no one would believe me over her. But when she came in tonight and told me what she wanted, I couldn't go along with it." Kay began to cry. "She said just for a couple of months and then it would end. She didn't tell me she would hurt her. I couldn't let that happen, so I fought her, but she got me."

"Who?"

She gasped. "Iona."

"Where is she?"

Nikki felt a gun pressed to the back of her head.

"She's right behind you," a familiar voice said.

Chapter 20

Nikki didn't turn and kept her voice calm. "Where's Callia?"

"You'll find out in a minute." Iona motioned her gun at Kay. "Help me tie her up." She dropped some rope next to Nikki.

Kay began to tremble. "Iona, please don't—"

"Keep your mouth shut and I won't kill you. I'm still debating that." She nudged Nikki. "Go."

Nikki tied Kay's hands.

"Make it tighter," Iona said. "I want to see her hands turn white."

Nikki tightened the rope, but as she made the knots, she inconspicuously loosened them again.

"Now do her feet."

Nikki repeated the same tactic she'd used with Kay's hands.

Iona pulled something out of her pocket and tossed it at her. "Now, cover her mouth."

Nikki complied.

"Good. Now let's get out of here." Iona went to Callia's bookshelf and hit a knob. A door opened, and she gestured Nikki to go through it, then turned to Kay. "I'll be back for you," she said, then closed the door.

She pushed Nikki down a hidden staircase. Once they reached the bottom, Nikki saw a tunnel and realized that it was likely one of the caves that led to a secret entrance into the house. It must have been a gold mine discovery for Alana and her family. They would have easily been able to hide and smuggle things into the house and get to their escape route on the beach. They had direct access without being seen.

"I slept with the architect," Iona said, as though reading Nikki's mind. "Lucian thinks no one knows about these secret passages, but I do. I know where the panic room is and other 'secret' areas. I knew them even back then. Although most of the mansion was burned by fire, the old structure remained intact, and the new builder just built around it. I got him to show me the old hidden entrances and some new ones."

Nikki didn't have time to question, because when she turned to Iona, something hit her and everything went black.

Basilio woke to stare into the emerald eyes of the devil. It took him a second to realize that the eyes belonged to his brother, but it didn't make the expression any less terrifying.

"What did you tell her?" Lucian said in a low voice.

"Who?"

"Iona," Dante said. He stood several feet behind Lucian.

Basilio scrambled up and stared at them. "What are you two talking about?"

"Callia's missing," Dante said.

"And I can't find Nikki, either," Lucian added. "Now, what did you tell her?"

Basilio rubbed his eyes. "What would Iona have to—"

Lucian grabbed his brother's T-shirt. "Don't play stupid with me. We've been watching Iona, tracking her steps. Watching her moves. Gauging her. We had everything planned to snare her, but something spooked her to act out of character and rush things." Lucian released his grip and stepped back. "What did you say to her?"

Basilio started to stand. "Let me talk to her."

Dante shook his head. "She's gone."

"What do you mean, she's gone?"

"No more questions," Lucian said. "Tell us about last night."

"I just confronted her about the dress."

"What dress?" Lucian asked.

"The dress Nikki first wore. I'd seen it in Iona's bedroom before."

"If you suspected anything, you should have come to me."

"I wanted to make sure. I didn't want to accuse her without hearing her side."

"But you knew she was the one behind it?"

"It just came to me. When I confronted her, she told me that someone else had given it to her to hem."

"And you believed her?"

"I had no reason not to."

"What else made you suspicious?" Lucian asked, reading his brother's hesitation.

"I didn't say anything, but I was just thinking about the night of the fire."

"What about it?"

Basilio lowered his head and shook it.

Lucian lifted his chin. "We don't have time for your silence. Two lives are at stake."

"Iona was with me. I mean, I left Callia alone in the hotel and went to a club. I didn't think it would be a problem. I met Iona and we went to bed. I woke up the next day and she was beside me and Callia was gone. I never suspected she had anything to do with it. She made me feel that she'd stand by me and keep my secret. That's all I thought about, not disappointing you. I didn't make the connection until recently, and I started putting certain pieces together. But I thought there wasn't enough time for her to take Callia to the island and then come back. She told me she was with me all night."

"You brainless idiot!" Dante said, exploding with anger.

"Dante," Lucian warned.

Dante ignored him. "She lies! You were passed out drunk or maybe even drugged. You have no idea what she could have done."

"I never thought she could—"

"And because you don't think about anyone but your-self, this is the second time you've put Callia's life in danger. And now Nikki's. What are we to say to her sister if we don't get to her in time?"

"We will," Lucian said in a quiet but lethal tone.

Dante gestured to Basilio in disgust. "No thanks to him."

Basilio jumped to his feet. "I didn't know!"

"I told you to stay away from her," Lucian said.

Basilio turned away. "Why didn't you trust me? Tell me something?"

"And how could I trust you when you didn't trust me? For all I knew, you were both in it together."

Basilio looked at his brother. "I would never—"

"I didn't know that. Your precious secret meant more than anything I said to you. The more I warned you, the closer you got to her."

"I loved her."

"I know. You loved her enough to want to marry her. It blinded you to everything. Before coming to your room, we discovered Kay bound and bleeding in Callia's room. She was one of Iona's victims, too, except Iona used the allure of money with her. She told us how Iona had bragged about becoming a rich woman. Kay's in custody now."

"It doesn't make sense. Why would she want to hurt Callia or anyone?"

"That's not the right question to ask right now. Where do you think she is?" Lucian said.

"There's a cave by the cove that she used to go to."

The three men raced out of the mansion and down to the cove. As they neared the opening of one of the caves, they halted and Dante studied the ground. "There are no fresh marks. She may not be here."

"Maybe she's left the island," Basilio said.

"No, she's taken them underground. Kay says she knows the tunnels well," Lucian said.

"She's right." Basilio stepped forward. "Look, let me—"

Lucian stopped him. "No. You're going to go back to the house and do what you do best."

"What's that?"

"Smile and lie," Dante said.

Basilio scowled at him, but Lucian spoke up before he could reply. "Yes, you're going to make sure that our guests don't suspect anything is wrong. If they ask questions, you tell them what they need to hear. Nothing else. Now go."

"I think I should help—"

"Go." Lucian's voice grew hard. "Don't disobey me this time."

Basilio swore, then spun away and marched off.

Dante watched him go. "Do you think we can trust him?"

"Now that he's no longer blind? Yes."

"You have more faith in him than I do."

"I know, but he's not the problem."

Now, waking again, the only thing Nikki knew was that she was in one of the caves. She had no idea how far underground they were, but knew that it wouldn't be an easy escape. She straightened and sat up and saw Callia sitting a few yards away from her. She looked scared, and Nikki felt as if she was trapped in one of her nightmares. Someone she loved was in trouble but out of reach. Unfortunately, this one was real, and unlike in her tormenting dreams, Nikki knew she couldn't fail. She couldn't live with that.

She tried to assess her surroundings—the cave was narrow, and she heard the sound of rushing water and knew there was a river cutting through it. She could jump in, but she didn't know where it would lead. She'd have to come up with something else.

"I knew you'd be a problem," Iona said, her voice echoing against the cave walls.

Nikki glanced at Callia. "Do you want a ransom?"

"No."

"Then what do you want?"

"I want brave Lucian to come down and get her and I'll be waiting for him."

"He'll come for me. You don't need her, too. Let her go."

Iona shoved her face into Nikki's. "When will you learn that I don't take orders? Especially from you." She straightened. "Alana could tell me anything. She was beautiful, pure, royal, not a mixed-blood mutt like you. I nearly laughed when I saw you in her dress. You were such a pitiable imitation. I wanted everyone to see that. And they did. Especially Lucian."

Nikki saw the look in her eyes and heard the anger and anguish in her voice. "Why do you hate him so much?"

"It's nothing personal."

"Then what is it?" Nikki asked, perplexed. "Is this because you think he killed Alana? He didn't."

"I know. I did." She turned away. "I didn't want to, but she forced me to."

"How can that be? What did she do to you?"

"I worshipped her," Iona spat out. "With my heart, my soul and my life. Alana understood me. All my life I've been tossed aside. My parents put me in an orphanage. I was adopted by a family who farmed me out to do household work and then kept my pay. I lived hand to mouth for years. No one cared. I was invisible and didn't matter. I, who have the looks to be a queen, was treated like nothing, like less than a slave. Men wanted me only to service them and never offered more. I learned early that it's best to use others before they use you. Then I came here and worked and didn't care that I was invisible like the rest. I was left alone to work and the money was good. Then Alana arrived, and do you know what she did?"

Nikki shook her head, afraid to speak.

"She smiled at me and made me her personal assistant. She let me choose her clothes for her, and when she traveled, she took me with her. She gave me clothes that she didn't want to wear anymore, and I kept every last one. She also gave me jewelry and gifts she'd gotten bored with. At last someone understood me. She taught me how to eat at a banquet, how to walk and present myself. She treated me like an equal and at last I felt that I could aspire to the life that I deserved.

"I knew that she was marrying Lucian for his money and she told me how she'd managed to seduce him. She also told me about her cousin's activities, and sometimes I would do a run for them. We were as close as sisters and she made me hope again. She made me realize that I could also snag a wealthy man and live the same life she did. I knew my opportunity had come when Basilio arrived. I could tell that he would be an easy conquest."

"He really loves you."

Iona laughed. "I know. The young ones are the easiest to manipulate."

"You didn't feel anything for him?"

"I cared for him as one would a beloved pet. That's one thing Alana taught me. Never fall in love with a man, or they control you. You must always have the upper hand."

"If you had such a close relationship, then why did you kill her?"

"Because she betrayed me. When I told her my plan regarding Basilio, she laughed. She laughed at me! She held her sides and laughed until tears streamed down her face. She said that my plan would never work. That Basilio would know better than to fall for a maid. That I was a nobody.

"In an instant she snatched away all my hope and stared at me like I was a dirty gold digger, though I was planning to do exactly what she had. But she said she had the class to do it. I didn't. I knew then that she'd stolen my only hope, so I did the same to her. She didn't deserve to be mistress of the Kontos mansion. I planted the bag of cocaine in a place I knew Callia would find it, and watched her careful strategy to marry Lucian and gain control of his island crumble. I watched her when Lucian forced her and her family off the island, and then I thought of my next step."

"For what?"

"To become mistress of the house."

Nikki stared, now remembering Iona's words. *You want to become mistress of it.*

"I overheard Lucian and Dante talking about their carefully orchestrated plan to burn down the mansion, and I knew the perfect way to make my dream come true. I sent Alana a message, as if it had come from Lucian. I took her to the secret entrance and told her that he'd heard about the baby and that was why he wanted to talk to her. I led her to the roof to wait for him. When he showed up, I let them talk, then fired. Unfortunately, she saw me and got in my way. I killed her, but only got him in the leg. I'd meant to kill them both, but my shots were off, so I went with my next plan. I left the roof and closed Lucian's escape route, so he was forced into the main house. I thought that would take care of him."

"And Callia?"

"Getting past Basilio was no trouble at all. I drugged his drink and then intercepted the hot chocolate that was delivered to Callia's room and drugged it as well. It was so easy to wait until she was knocked out. Then I carried her onto a boat I had waiting and took her to the island. No one saw us. I carried her to the house, went in through another secret entrance and placed her in her bedroom. I heard Dante and Lucian as they poured the accelerant, and I tried not to laugh, knowing the true torment Lucian was about to face. I expected the smoke to take her first."

"But you were wrong."

She frowned. "It should have worked."

"She was just a child. Why would you want to kill her?"

"Because with Callia and Lucian dead, everything would go to Basilio. He would be so distraught losing his family in the fire, he would turn to the first comforting arms that were there. I planned that to be me. We would marry and then I'd be mistress and no one would look down on me again."

"But Callia woke up."

"Yes, but I had another tactic that should have worked."

"Kay?"

"Yes, I thought that if I made Callia appear crazy, Lucian would have her put into an institution, and then I would plant evidence and arouse suspicion to get Lucian arrested for murdering Alana, and once again Basilio would have everything. It would have worked if you hadn't come along. At first you were perfect, because you have some similarities to Alana and could confuse the girl, but I soon realized you were dangerous to me."

194 *Secret Paradise*

"Dangerous?"

"Yes, you wanted this house."

"I wanted Lucian."

Iona ignored her. "You wanted to take Alana's place and I couldn't let that happen."

"Is that why you told me Lucian was a murderer?"

Iona shrugged. "I was spreading that rumor so that I could implicate him later, but I told you because I wanted you to be frightened and leave. I wanted you to doubt him. I couldn't let you get too close to him. But when you didn't leave, I knew I had to convince Basilio to marry me. Then there would be nothing Lucian could do, but he hesitated because you were confusing his mind with questions."

"You should have given up," Nikki said.

"I never give up," Iona shot back.

"But your two plans failed."

"I won't fail this time."

"You won't escape. They know all about you now."

"They may know about me, but it's too late. And they won't catch me. I know this island and I know these caves. I've studied them over the years. By the time I was rehired, I'd put my plan in action and I knew that no one suspected me." She gave a quick motion of her hand. "Get up. It's time to move." She blew out the light from the candle and turned on a torch. "Feel free to run. You'll never find your way out. Or you can just follow my light."

"You go first," Nikki said.

Iona shoved her forward. "Give me another order and I'll shove you in the river. Now move."

Nikki followed wherever Iona shone the light and felt Callia close behind her. Finally Iona shone the torch on an iron ladder bolted into the wall. Nikki knew this was her chance. A ladder pointing upward meant land. It meant a chance of escape.

"Callia, run!" she said. Then she shoved Iona hard.

She heard the gun clatter to the ground, then tried to dash toward the ladder. Iona got to her first, grabbing her hair and pulling her back. Nikki fought wildly, and soon they were both airborne, then falling into the water. Iona let go as the rushing water separated them, and Nikki sank into further darkness. Nikki didn't know up from down. She tried to reach the surface as the water began to carry her away, but kept hitting rocks. She knew she was trapped in a river tunnel and that she'd likely drown. She imagined that Callia was safe. And while that thought ended one nightmare, another had just begun.

Basilio stormed back to the house, feeling the weight of his shame. Dante was right. Twice he'd failed. He'd let a woman use him, lie to him and betray him. Callia's and Nikki's lives were in danger all because of him. They could… He vehemently shook his head. No, he couldn't think about it. He wouldn't let it happen. He wouldn't let Iona win. He paused when he heard running footsteps. He turned just as Callia ran into him, still looking behind her. He grabbed her and she screamed.

"It's okay," he said. "It's me."

She looked up at him, then behind her again. "Nikki saved my life."

"Where is she?"

"Iona has her. In the caves." She took his hand. "I'll show you where I came out from."

"Wait here. I'll be right back."

"No, I don't want to be alone."

"Fine. Come on."

With Callia in tow he ran back to the cove where his brother and the other men were discussing a strategy.

"I found Callia!"

They all turned and then Callia ran to Lucian.

"Are you all right?" he said, searching her for any injuries.

"Iona has Nikki."

Lucian nodded. "I know."

"She's not here," Callia said, looking around the cove. "Come on, before it's too late. I think I know where she is."

Callia led them to the tunnel from which she'd escaped. "She's still down there. I heard a splash."

"That means she won't be here," Lucian said, walking to another cave. "She'll be farther down."

Dante swore. "She'll be swept out to sea."

"Not if I get to her first," Lucian said.

Basilio shook his head, afraid for his brother. "You can't—"

"I know these tunnels, too, and I'm a strong swimmer." Lucian stopped in front of a cave that looked like an animal's burrow. It was tight and low to the ground. He'd have to crawl into it. "I have to at least try."

"But—"

"He's a great swimmer," Callia said with fierce support. "He'll save Nikki."

Lucian was glad to have her confidence. He knew the caves better than anyone. He knew where they turned and dropped and how the water flowed. It was still dangerous, and possibly a deadly choice, but he had to make it. The darkness didn't frighten him. He would rescue her. He got down on his knees, checked his pocket for his penlight, set his cane aside and then crept into darkness.

Chapter 21

It was a torturous, slow death. For fleeting moments Nikki felt herself being pushed toward the surface by the force of the water and given a chance for air. But she was always dragged down again, each time reaching out to grab something but always meeting emptiness. Soon the water settled, giving her a chance to emerge at the surface and gulp in air until her chest felt as if it would burst. She looked around, her eyes growing used to the darkness, but all she sensed were more walls. She swam to the edge and called out. Would anyone hear her? She knew they would be looking for her, but it was a large island with many caves and tunnels. They could be on the other side, for all she knew, but she couldn't think that way. She would make it out of there.

Suddenly she felt the water move. Something was coming. Oh God, Iona had found her. Nikki was pushing herself from the wall, ready to dive into the water again, when something grabbed her leg. She screamed and fought to free herself.

"Shh," Lucian said. "It's me. I've got you."

Nikki collapsed into his arms in disbelief. "I was so afraid no one would find me."

He held her close. "Now you don't have to be afraid anymore."

"It's so dark. How will we—"

"It's okay. Trust me. It will be a little rough, but we'll make it."

"Callia," Nikki said, remembering. "Have you found her?"

"Yes, she's safe, Artemis," he replied, using the nickname he'd first given her. "She helped let me know where I might find you. Come on."

"Can't we go back the way we came?"

"No, it's best not to fight the current. Don't worry. I know where this river leads. Just hold my hand and don't let go."

Nikki didn't let go, even when she feared the current would rip them apart and felt all her energy would fail her. She was determined that the water and the darkness wouldn't win. Soon the current weakened and then disappeared. She could feel that they were in a large opening and not just an air pocket.

Lucian stopped and lifted her up. "We'll get out here." He gestured ahead. "See that spot of light? I want you to crawl toward it."

"Is there a ladder?"

"No, not all tunnels were used or made by smugglers. This one nature made. Go on. I'll be right behind you."

Lucian watched her go and hesitated. He didn't want her to see him without his cane. He was nimble and strong in the water, but on land he could hardly walk without it. At one moment he felt like a hero and the next like a broken man. The darkness welcomed him.

"Lucian?" Nikki called out, anxiety and fear in her voice.

He reluctantly smiled, knowing she'd never let him stay in darkness. She would always be his light. "I'm coming."

Nikki hovered around the opening of the cave, waiting for Lucian to come out. But he was taking too long. Had something happened? Would she have to go back and get him? She was considering her options when he finally emerged. Nikki fell on her knees and hugged him. She swallowed hard and bit back tears of joy.

"We'll get the doctor to look at you," Lucian said. "Go on ahead."

Nikki shook her head. "I'm okay."

"You go ahead, anyway."

Nikki paused, knowing why he was trying to send her away. "I know you don't have your cane. Let me help you up."

"Please don't ask me to do that."

"I'm strong enough for you to lean on me. Don't be too proud." She lowered her voice. "A strong man knows his weakness, and a wise man his faults."

Lucian relented and allowed Nikki to help him rise. She grunted. "You weigh a ton," she teased.

He smiled, then his smile fell when he saw Iona standing in front of them with a gun.

"I wonder if I should shoot your other leg this time."

"You've lost, Iona," Lucian said.

"Not yet."

She had aimed, ready to shoot, when a dark form

jumped down from one of the trees and landed on her head. It attacked her face with its sharp claws, drawing blood. She screamed as Lethe assaulted her with all his animal fury. Nikki helped Lucian lean against a tree, then ran and grabbed the gun. Iona's screams alerted the others. Within minutes Lethe released her, but not before doing considerable damage to her face. Soon the patrol had her in handcuffs.

Nikki went over to Lucian and rested her head against him.

Dante joined them and said with a flourish, "Thank God that's over."

Callia hugged them. "I'm so glad you're all right."

"Yes," Nikki said as Lucian took the cane Dante handed him.

Dante glanced up and saw Basilio, who saw the butler's look of disdain and turned away.

"It's not his fault," Nikki said, seeing Dante's stern look.

"He was reckless, disobedient and stubborn."

"You just described me," Nikki said.

Dante shook his head. "You're different."

"Not really," Nikki said. "I understand him. He worships Lucian but also wants to be different than him. He wants to be seen as his own man. As a younger sibling, I know how important it is to have someone you admire be proud of you. Appreciate your accomplishments, even if they never measure up."

"Accomplishments?" Dante said with a sniff. "He hasn't tried to accomplish anything, and to be with Iona, a woman—"

"When did you know about her?" Nikki asked.

"A while ago," Lucian said, "but I suspected more when the head wrap turned up. Callia mentioned it, and I knew no one would have something from Ghana except Iona, to whom, I knew, Alana had given most of her throwaways."

"Iona thought they were gifts," Nikki revealed.

"Alana didn't give gifts. Iona may as well have been a trash bin. Once Alana was finished with something, whether it was an item or a person, she had no use for it," Lucian said. "I wanted to see what role my brother was playing in her deception, before I made my move," he added.

"She chose the perfect mark," Dante said.

"Why don't you like him?" Nikki asked, surprised by Dante's level of disgust. "Yes, he's young, and yes, he was taken in, but if you look past his mistakes, you'll see that you two have a lot in common."

Dante pointed to himself. "Me?"

"Yes. You're both willing to protect those you care about." Nikki waved his protest away. "I know he tried to protect the wrong person."

"You mean himself? He didn't do it for Iona. He lied because he didn't want Lucian to know what really happened."

"Do you blame him?" Lucian said.

"Give him another chance and you'll uncover how you're both very much the same," Nikki added.

Dante shook his head. "No, we're not."

"You're both good-looking, charming in your own ways and considerate. If you gave him a chance, you could be friends," Nikki said.

Dante shuddered. "No, never that."

Lucian sent him a look. "But perhaps something else."

Dante paused. "Does he have to know?"

Lucian nodded. "I think it's time. He's heartbroken.

There's nothing you can say that he won't say to himself. Forgive him for being young and reckless and for falling in love with the wrong woman. He's not the only one."

"Does he have to know what?" Nikki asked, but both men ignored her question.

Dante lit a cigarette and sighed. "I suppose I do owe Basilio for one thing."

"What?" Nikki asked.

He offered her one of his rare smiles. "Bringing you into our lives."

Chapter 22

"Are you sure you don't want to come back with us?" Monica asked her sister as she packed her suitcase.

She and J.D. had stayed an extra three days to be with Nikki while Lucian traveled to the mainland to talk to the police. Callia and Nikki had also spoken to them and given their statements, but Lucian had made sure the meeting was brief, and with his influence the officers followed his orders and were soon gone.

Strangely, despite their horrendous ordeal, Callia had recovered quickly. She didn't have any nightmares and her mood seemed oddly buoyant. It was when Nikki saw Callia putting a flower in a vase that she discovered the reason why.

"Dante and I are friends again. We sat on the beach and talked like we did in the old days, and today Dante gave this to me. My favorite flower, which he picked up from a vendor on the mainland."

Nikki looked at the variety of flowers that sur-rounded her in the house and even beyond, in the garden. She knew that to Callia none of them mattered. "It's beautiful."

"Yes, it's my favorite color, too, red. He told me that he's so glad that I'm safe and how brave I was to escape and lead them back to the cave, and then he handed me this."

Nikki bit her lip, tempted to warn Callia not to make too much of it, but she didn't want to remove the joy on the young woman's face in the slightest way. She de-served this recaptured happiness.

"I know it's nothing much," Callia said, as if Nikki had spoken aloud. "But I'll keep it forever, because it means that just for a moment, he was thinking of me."

"That's right."

Callia smelled the flower and sighed. "I'm so glad we're friends again."

"Yes."

She sent Nikki a coy look. "And in a few years I'll convince him that we can be a lot more."

Nikki couldn't help a smile. It seemed clear that Callia was quickly heading toward womanhood and would soon learn the power of her looks and the mas-tery of feminine charm.

Nikki thought of that now as she sat on the bed and watched her sister close up her suitcase. Dante's gift and Callia's happiness had given her an idea. "I do need your help," she said, jumping off the bed.

"With what?"

"I need you to help me pack."

"You've decided to come with us? Not that I blame you. You've been through a lot and need a break from this place."

"Come on. I don't want Lucian to see me."

"Why not?" Monica asked as she followed her sister to her room.

Nikki entered her bedroom and pulled out her suitcase.

"You can't just leave without saying goodbye."

Nikki opened her armoire. "That's right. I need to leave him a note."

"I think you should say what you want to say in person."

"Not yet. I need you and J.D. to do something for me."

"Anything."

Nikki told Monica what she'd planned, and as Monica listened, a smile spread on her face.

Basilio sat in Lucian's study, wondering why Lucian had called the meeting. It had been over a week since the event with Iona, and his brother had barely spoken to him. Not that there had been much time. Lucian had spent lots of time on the mainland and then a few days ago he'd taken Dante and Callia and gone on a trip with Nikki, Monica and J.D. to his home in England, because Monica had asked him to. He'd invited Basilio to join them, but Basilio felt like an outsider and offered to stay behind.

But he didn't stay on the island. Instead he rented a room on the mainland and drank himself into a pitying stupor for a few days, until he realized he was being stupid. He was an outsider because of his own stupidity. He liked life to be easy and whined whenever it wasn't. When his mother died, he'd gone to Lucian for help. When he needed work, he turned to Lucian to give it to him. Not once had he given his brother anything. That was why he'd worked with Monica to get Nikki to come and redesign the place. And she'd made the place great and made his brother happy, and he'd nearly ruined it.

Basilio ended his pity party, ready to prove to his brother that he hadn't made a mistake by letting him stay. He would run the villas and make sure that everything was in order. He would come up with ideas. See what other holdings his brother had and see how he could help. Maybe Lucian would let him oversee one of his investments or businesses and give him the opportunity to make it even more successful. He felt a new ambition filling him. He would never be some woman's pansy again.

Now Lucian was back, J.D. and Monica were heading back home and his brother had ordered to see him. What did his brother want to say to him? Was he going to tell him to leave? He looked over at Dante, who stood by the corner. Did his brother have to shame him in front of that bastard? He didn't want to have to plead with him to give him another chance, but he would, because it wasn't just that Lucian was the only immediate family he had left. He loved him. His brother meant everything to him.

He couldn't blame Lucian for wanting to send him away. He'd probably do the same. He knew he could find a job somewhere else, but it wouldn't be the same. He'd miss everything here. He was a different man now. Hell, he even liked cats. After seeing what Lethe had done to Iona, he'd thought of getting one for himself. But it wasn't just that he'd changed; this place, Callia, Nikki and Lucian had become his home and family, and he didn't want to give them up.

"I'm sorry to keep you waiting," Lucian said, coming into his study and walking over to his desk.

"I know I messed up," Basilio said, ready to defend himself. "And you have every right to be angry with me—"

"You're forgiven," Lucian interrupted.

Basilio stopped, with his mouth open. He closed it and stared at his brother a moment. "What?"

"That's not why I asked to see you."

Basilio shifted in his seat. "Why then?"

"I thought we should have an official family reunion."

Basilio jerked his finger at Dante. "Then why the hell is he here?"

"Because he's family."

Basilio rose to his feet. "What?"

"He's our half brother."

"Is this a joke?"

Dante folded his arms. "No."

"He knows why we never saw Dad again," Lucian said.

Basilio turned to Dante, then back to Lucian. "Do I really want to hear this?"

Dante shrugged. "It's up to you. If you're too scared—"

Basilio spun to him. "I'm not scared of anything."

"Stop taunting him," Lucian said. "Tell him."

Dante sighed and let his hands fall to his sides. "Our father liked to juggle women. My mother met him after your mother. She didn't know about her when she married him."

"Our father was a bigamist?"

"A polygamist."

"There were more?"

"Two more."

Basilio collapsed into his seat and covered his eyes. "I don't believe this."

"Well, he juggled his women well until one found out about the other and—"

"Killed him?"

"It was never proven," Lucian said.

"My mother learned about Lucian and the connection to my father and encouraged me to contact him. I needed the work, so I did," Dante said.

Basilio looked at Lucian, amazed. "How many more secrets do you have?"

Lucian sent him a level stare. "Hopefully no more than you."

Basilio sighed and held up his hands. "None. I have no secrets to keep."

"Good. Me too."

"Me three," Dante said. "This doesn't change anything. I still think you're a brainless dummy."

Basilio frowned. "And you're an officious idiot."

Dante held out his hand. "But I'd prefer you as a brother than as an enemy."

Basilio shook it. "Agreed."

Lucian stood. "Good. Now, which one of you will help me choose a ring? The idiot or the dummy?"

Dante jerked his head at Lucian and looked at Basilio. "What do you think we should call him?"

"Nothing that he'll let us get away with."

Dante laughed. "You're right."

Lucian leaned back in his chair. "You haven't answered my question."

Basilio rubbed his hands together. "So you're going to make it official with Nikki?"

Lucian glanced at his watch. "I have the jeweler scheduled for this time." There was a knock on the door.

"Come in," Lucian said, and the jeweler came in and laid out his selection.

"Don't you want to wait a few days?" Dante said, ever cautious.

"I think he should seize the moment," Basilio said, eager to help his brother make the right choice. "Don't let her get away."

Chapter 23

With a ring chosen, Lucian went to Nikki's room, ready to surprise her. He knocked on the door, then opened it. He stopped when he saw the sight before him. Her bed was made and all her things were gone. He turned when he heard footsteps and saw Callia stroking Pauline as she walked down the hall.

"Have you seen Nikki?" he asked her.

"I saw her going with Monica and J.D. to the helicopter."

"Was she carrying bags?"

"Yes," Callia said slowly. "I thought they were her sister's." She placed Pauline on the floor. "Why? What's wrong?"

"I'm sure it's nothing."

Callia pushed past him and looked in the room. "She's taken everything! She's gone without saying goodbye."

Lucian patted her shoulder. "Don't get upset. I'm sure there's a reason. Go. I'll figure out what's going on."

"She wouldn't leave us like this."

Lucian smiled and turned away. She would. She had. She'd taken her things and gone. Maybe it had all been too much for her. He took the ring out of his pocket and stared at it. He'd been as foolish as poor Benjamin. She wasn't a woman a man could hope to pin down.

"Well, what did she say?" Basilio said when he met Lucian in the foyer.

"She's not here," Lucian said, walking past him to go to the terrace.

"She has to be here."

"But she's not."

"Where is she, then?"

"She's just taking her sister to the mainland," Dante said, overhearing them. "It was arranged."

Lucian took a seat. "Was it also arranged that she take all her things with her?"

Dante hesitated, taken aback by the question. "No. But she wouldn't—"

"It seems she has. She's gone."

"There must be some sort of mistake."

"There's no mistake."

Basilio swore. "Women." He got the attention of one of the servants and said, "Get me a drink."

Dante lit up a cigarette.

Lucian watched them and wondered which vice he should take up. He held his hand out to Dante. "Give me one," he said, nodding to the cigarette.

"You don't smoke."

"That's not the point."

"I don't trust you with matches."

Lucian lifted an eyebrow. "Are you trying to be funny?"

"I'm not giving you a cigarette. It's not a habit you should start."

"You can't stop me."

"No, but you can buy your own pack."

Callia raced out. "Uncle Lucian! Uncle Lucian!"

He sat up. "What?"

She waved a piece of paper. "She left you a note. I found it in her room." She handed it to him.

Lucian rubbed his eyebrow and stared at it.

"Open it, for goodness' sakes," Basilio said with impatience.

"I will."

When Lucian didn't move to open it, Basilio said, "Let me read it if you don't want to. I'm used to bad news."

"How do you know it's bad?" Callia said.

"He doesn't," Dante replied. "Lucian, read it when you're ready."

Basilio snatched the note. "He's ready now."

Dante took it from him. "No, he's not."

"Careful," Callia cried. "You'll rip it."

Lucian held out his hand. "It's mine and I'll read it."

Dante gave the note to him, and they all waited as he carefully unfolded it and read it.

"Well?" Basilio said when his brother remained silent.

He handed it to him.

"'I hope you won't be angry with me,'" Basilio read, "'but I couldn't help myself. I did it, anyway.'" He looked at Lucian, confused. "Did what, anyway?"

Lucian shrugged. "I don't know."

"I hate riddles."

Dante took the note. "That's because they force you to think. I'm sure there's a clue in here."

Basilio folded his arms, smug. "Bet you can't figure it out, either."

"What would Nikki want to do for you?" Callia asked.

Lucian shook his head, stumped. What else was there that she thought would upset him? She'd done everything for him, and he hadn't made any part of his life off-limits except... "I think I know what she means," he said and headed inside.

"What?" Basilio asked as they all followed him.

Lucian didn't reply until he reached his bedroom. Then he stopped and said, "Wait," as Callia began to open the door. "I can do this." He took a deep breath, then opened it. It was just as he'd suspected. Nikki had redesigned his bedroom. There was no more darkness, but bright sunlight filtered in, covering the new flooring and furniture. He stood amazed by all of it, but what caught his attention most was Nikki, who lay on the bed in a silk two-piece with rose petals surrounding her.

She sat up when she saw them. "Oh, I didn't expect an audience."

Lucian stepped into the room and shamelessly closed the door behind him so that they could be alone. "Now your audience is only me."

"It was tricky getting this done. I drew a quick sketch, then had everything shipped in and stored while we were in England. Then, while you were in your office, I had to get everything into place."

Lucian approached the bed. "Hmm."

"How do you like the room?" Nikki asked, a little uneasy with his silence.

His gaze swept over her body. "It's nice."

"Nice? It's more than nice. You're not even looking at it."

"I am," he said, his gaze never leaving her. "I really like the bed."

"Really?"

"Yes, I like how you put yourself in the middle of it."

"I thought you might. Check the closet."

He halted. "Why?"

"Just do it."

Lucian went over to the closet and opened it, to see Nikki's clothes hanging alongside his.

"We'll eventually need more closet space," Nikki said.

"Clearly."

"Do you like your surprise?"

He took the ring out of his pocket. "Only if you want to make it official."

Nikki stared at the beautiful symphony of stones.

"I'm not getting down on one knee," Lucian said.

Nikki held out her hand. "I didn't expect you to." She wiggled her fingers and he slid the ring on. "So are you going to ask me?"

"Do I have to?"

"Yes."

"Will you marry me?"

She playfully bit her lip. "Can I think about it?"

Lucian raised both eyebrows. "Do I look like Benjamin?"

"Definitely not."

Lucian unbuttoned his shirt. "You have thirty seconds, or I'll withdraw my offer."

"You drive a hard bargain."

He tossed his shirt on the floor. "I've been told I can be ruthless."

Nikki undid his trousers. "But not with me."

"No, never with you." He removed his trousers and climbed on top of her. "So, what's your answer?"

Nikki stared up at him and slid her hand down his thigh. "My answer all depends on you."

"Me?"

"Yes. Do you love me?"

Lucian paused, and a black river of fear swept through Nikki as his silence lingered. She feared that she'd asked too much of him. That once again she'd ruined a sacred moment between them and broken a bond. That the light in his eyes would grow dim and the wall that had been slowly falling around his heart would start to go back up. But Lucian cupped the side of her face, his eyes a radiant green, which had her hypnotized, and when he finally spoke, his voice had a tenderness she had never heard before.

"You once told me that love was like water." His thumb brushed gently against her lower lip and his voice deepened. "But if I could own every sea, river and ocean in this world, it still would not be enough to hold the love I feel for you."

Nikki was too overcome with sweet joy to form any words, so she just threw her arms around him and held him close.

"Callia knew you would stay."

"She has a special gift." Nikki raised her voice an octave. "I'll let her help me select my wedding dress."

They both smiled when they heard a yelp of pleasure behind the closed door, but neither left the room for a very long time.

* * * * *

REQUEST YOUR FREE BOOKS!

2 FREE NOVELS
PLUS 2 FREE GIFTS!

KIMANI™
ROMANCE

Love's ultimate destination!

Harlequin® *Desire*

ALWAYS POWERFUL, PASSIONATE AND PROVOCATIVE.

NEW YORK TIMES **AND** *USA TODAY*
BESTSELLING AUTHOR

BRENDA JACKSON

**PRESENTS A BRAND-NEW
WESTMORELAND FAMILY NOVEL!**

FEELING THE HEAT

Their long-ago affair ended abruptly and
Dr. Micah Westmoreland knows Kalena Daniels
hasn't forgiven him. But now that they're working
side by side, he can't ignore the heat between them…
and this time he plans to make her his.

Also available as a 2-in-1 that includes
Night Heat.

Available in April wherever books are sold.